T5-BBA-658

A Lavish
of Sin

A Lavish
of Sin

Carlton E. Morse

Seven Stones Press

Woodside, California

A special thank you to Vance Randolph and George P. Wilson for *Down In The Holler,* a picturesque dictionary of Ozark Speech. It was used without reserve.

ISBN 0-940249-02-2

Cover and book design by David Charlsen

Cover illustration by Michael Pearce

For additional copies of this book check your local bookstore, or you may write directly to the publisher:

Seven Stones Press
Star Route Box 50
Woodside, CA 94062

Please enclose $14.95 per copy plus $1.50 for shipping and handling. California residents please add appropriate sales tax.

Dedicated to
Dr. Ernest Chastain
who recognizes and loves a good story
more than anyone

A Lavish
of Sin

PROLOGUE

Hal Morgan Jr. Sums Up

March, 1955

I began to awaken to my background when I was nine, which was when Grandma Peebler had her feet washed for the last time by Tom Starr to honor her God, and then went to her reward. In my heart I hope it was a joyous reward and not a just one; for if she got as good as she gave, I fear she is having a pretty rough time of it.

I was at the end of my twelfth year when Tom blew up the Trap Door to Hell up on the Ridge and was found drowned in Salt Creek next day by Max Shoemaker. I was approaching fourteen when they buried Eve Corvell, Marvin Culbertson came home from medical school to replenish his grubstake, and Bert Sweeney and I broke into his root cellar laboratory and were sick at what we saw there.

Even though fifteen years have now added weight and balance to my sensibilities, since Wayne's tragic demise and my mother's dying up there on the Summit en route to Kalispell, I still cannot look back upon these events without a kind of inner bleeding.

These fifteen years, devoted to laying down a medical background for my approach to the field of psychiatry, have given me greater understanding and have changed morbidity

1

to wholesome sympathy. Nevertheless, as son and brother to such naked tragedies, I still have moments of deep and bitter resentment against a society which permits its people to be molded into such caricatures of the beautiful human animal which nature, in the first place, had created.

Here I would like to say a good word for the Rev. Mr. Grocer, for he was an honest man and an earnest one. In all fairness his tenets had no common ground with the fever and fervor which made a tyrant of my grandmother and a sort of simple religious idiot of Old Tom. Mr. Grocer did the best he knew with the limited mental and spiritual equipment which was given him. My criticism of him and all Reverend gentlemen of his ilk, is the charge of futile inadequacy. His flock wanted realistic answers to their very real earthly problems. They asked for spiritual bread to sustain them; he could only give them stale unnourishing crumbs of cant and ritual. They sought a relief from their dreary, meaningless, daily drudgery; all he could offer was the added burden of moral restraints. They sought positive enlightment, immediate relief; he had nothing but negative promises of life after death in his bag of tricks.

A good man; an earnest man; a completely ineffectual man.

My father is dead. When he sold the Grizzly Flat ranch he divided the money evenly between himself and me and gave my share to Marvin for my education. It was generous.

Following the sale of Grizzly Flat, I saw nothing of him until his body was returned to me. He had become a wandering man and a recluse. His remains were found in a tiny shack deep in the Canadian Rockies wilderness. Death was said to be from natural causes; which in my own mind meant a broken heart. He had loved Wayne above us all.

Now just a word about Marvin Culbertson, Doctor Culbertson these past eleven years. There is a medical center in the Yaates now, down alongside the Federal Building. The midwives from the Ridge are never called upon any more. Neither are the children of our unmarried girls any longer sent up to the baby farms. Dr. Culbertson has made this his life work and has taken much of the shame and nonsense out of a natural life function, to the salvation of the girls and the improvement of Montana's infant mortality rate.

Jennie Loughner is sixty-two now and hasn't changed with the years. Her hair may have greyed a little but her face is still as smooth and fresh and full of character as the day I first saw her. She and Marvin see much of each other. I have always wondered whether Marvin and she ever came to any verbal understanding concerning their true relationship. Somehow I don't think so. I don't think Jennie would ever allow the stigma of her past to touch this fine man, whom she so wholeheartedly adores. However, I am convinced that Marvin in his secret heart knows he is her son. I don't know why I feel this; he has never hinted at it.

PART I

Chili Winneger: Hired Girl

June, 1934

When Grandma Eliza Peebler took to her bed at eighty-six, Chili Winneger came to work a spell for the Morgans and stayed five years. She "Seen at once the old lady's blight on her daughter, Sarah, and the whole Morgan tribe, and rode it out like a tick on the furry hide of death."

Chili was the only hired girl in Yaates Valley; a sloppy, rump-sprung, string-haired woman of forty-seven who had three unbridled pendulums, one of which was her tongue.

In the beginning Sarah Morgan had tried to put her in a brassiere. Chili said she harnessed the blamed contraption on, but you might as well try to keep a pair of gopher snakes in a string bag.

It was a surprise to everyone that the tightlipped Mrs. Morgan tolerated Chili in her house, her being the loose mouth she was. Romeo McFeddor thought maybe Mrs. Morgan got some relief hearing Chili say the things she wouldn't let herself even think. Romeo thought further that Mrs. Morgan was cup-full of the "Thou Shalt Nots" inherited from her tyrant mother.

Hal Morgan Senior couldn't abide Chili. "She rattltybangs in one spot doing the same job seven times and always where you want her least, her mouth going thirteen to the dozen.

"I once seen her stand polishing a stove lid ten minutes straight, after she had it shined to shame the noon sun. No wonder cookstoves got wore out in this cabin! And all the time she was talking the lining out of my earbone."

Chili's flow of monologues were colorful and sometimes a little hard to follow. They were invariably on the subject of one of her three husbands. She said her first man, Ace Younger, died of "wrecktle" injuries on the Columbia highway just south of Wenatchee. The other driver was drunk as two judges, but it's like scratchin' a poor man's ass to get money out of an insurance company.

Her second husband, Jack Lucey, had a "hearty" condition. "My family warned me the sign was on him, but he kept settin' up to me, and one night he talked me into it before I could git word to God. I sure drove my hogs to an empty trough when I married Jack Lucey. The man just wasn't up to it. He tried to cut a big hawg with a little knife and died of a conniption fit on our honeymoon.

"Us Fenton women is different clay. We're hard to tear down. But I really let my skimmer leak when I married Willy Winneger and come to live on a stump farm here in the Yaates; Willy is slow as pond water and never could find his butt with both hands. I tried to quit him, but Pa told me I'd married the man, so go back and set on the blister. We et wild rabbits until Willy'd dive for a brush pile every time he heard a dog bark. The cupboard got so empty, we looked at each other to see who we'd eat first. Then Old Lady Peebler come ailing, and that's when I come to scrub for Miz Morgan."

Chili sometimes talked about putting Willy in an "institution for the Mindful." She didn't know whether it was the mountain liquor up on the Ridge or the girls that was making Willy absent-minded. He'd shod the horse all around on both scores, and she'd had just about all of him she could chamber.

Actually Chili spent her Sunday off with Willy, and week after week she'd come back to the ranch either with a black eye, a bruised face or a black-and-blue mark on her throat, and always she'd "run into a door" down at Willy's shack. She told this story to Romeo McFeddor on an occasion.

"Why don't you tear off that Goddamn door," he advised, "before it knocks your brains out or strangles you to death?"

Romeo told Seth Bascomb he'd been up at Willy's cabin a couple of times, and the corn Willy and Chili lapped up on a Sunday would float a Pend Oreille trout. And the row that went on inside would pass for the Second Coming.

One time he'd heard Chili a-screeching, fit for wildcats and Willy yelling bloody murder, and he took a peek in the window. Chili had Willy down and a-straddle him, hittin' him in the face with her two fists, and his first thought was that this was the end of Willy; then he seen what was really on the fire, and he snuck away on account a man and wife should not be disturbed worshipping at the hymeneal altar, even if both parties were drunk as catnip kittens. They was like pigs after a punkin.

Romeo said everybody know'd how Willy was. Willy maintained, "This mountain whiskey was three times twisted and so good you could hardly bite it off."

Romeo admitted it was so strong you could smell the feet of the boys that plowed the corn, but nobody had to make a human hogstead out of hisself. Anyway, it looked like Chili was equal to him; maybe even the better man.

"Once Willy'd come tearing out of the shack ahead of a scalding coffee pot, mentioning Hell at every jump; if he'd had a feather in his hand, you could have called it flying."

Chili was sober, sedate, bright and early back in the Morgan kitchen of a Monday morning, usually as full of hum and buzz as a bee in a hive. She was effervescent with snatches of tunes, bits of song and good humor: "Redwing," "Turkey in the Straw," "Red River Valley" and "Casey Jones," to mention a few. This was the one day of the week she didn't have much to say against Willy.

But Sarah kept Chili on, and Hal put up with it just as he put up with everything else his wife and ancient crone of a mother-in-law set their minds to.

Still he did wonder what Chili was for when Mrs. Morgan went around after her, doing everything all over again to her own satisfaction. Chili dusted the furniture, Sarah dusted; Chili moved a chair, Sarah put it back to the very inch; Chili swamped out the kitchen or made a bed; Sarah was right behind her to "put it to rights." It made even Chili fidgety.

"Honest to Grandma, Miz Morgan, honey," she said good-naturedly, "if you don't stop traipsin' around in my footsteps doin' over what I've already did twice, I'm gonna throw in the towel. You'll have me thinking about my work, you keep on like this."

"Maybe you'd do better work if you did think," Sarah suggested.

"No, Ma'am, I wouldn't do it at all! When I think about work, I just can't stomach it. I get all wore out before I start. But if I can get to thinking about Ace of Jack or Willy, my hackles ruffle up, and I'm so fermenting with get up and git, I can clean house like Grandpa Jenks a-stompin' out a grassfire in his beard."

Chili Talks and Talks

That just about explained Chili as completely as anyone could; why she jumped up and down in one place so long; why she was always talking . . . she called it thinking out loud. Like the time Chili went in to turn Grandma Peebler over to rest her bones and stayed an hour rubbing the old creature's back and poured into Grandma's wandering mind how she came to marry her first husband.

"I was a gander-eyed fourteen down in Tennessee and pretty as a new-laid egg when I married Ace," she reported to the deaf old ears. "I never rightly could figure why I done it, ceptin' I was so brightly burning in them days you'd of thought Hell was a mile away and all the fences down. The young boys was a-draggin' their wings in the dust thicker'n whores at a funeral. My Ma said our front yard looked like it was fixing to swarm. Seems I took to Ace on account my folks didn't.

"He was a thin and ready feller, tall as a well rope and made a girl's skirttail pop at the dancing. In them days I was struttin' like a chicken in high barley.

"Soon as we married, though, I lost my smart ideas like beads off a string. He took me to a shack the wind blowed through like a corncrib. Our cupboards was as empty as a dead man's eyes, and in no time I was sorry as a toad under a disc harrow; that man was lazy as a shingle maker, all vines and no 'taters. Inside a year I was buzzard-ragged and down

9

to one shift of clothes, so out at the elbows you'd a-thought I'd been sortin' wild cats. Ace always did look like the dogs had got 'im under the cabin after he married me and give up work. My family sure was disgusted.

"First year we moved west my Pa got him three jobs; on an apple farm out of Wenatchee, then in a cannery cullin' fruit, and after that a plow job in the big wheat country over out of Spokane. Ace tried 'em on for size and then said he'd rather put on a tin bill and pick manure with the chickens. He was drinking a lot of mountain dew and that made him ornery. Always went around with his stinger about half out.

"Ace's own folks was disappointed in him something awful the way he'd gone back on his raising. That first winter in Washington it was so cold the wolves was eating sheep for the wool. We sure did have a miserable time what with the holes in the roof, the chinking out of the walls, and me having a baby and my milk drying up from too much moonlight, 'stead of bread in my mouth. The only wet nurse we could afford was so ugly we had to blindfold the baby before it would suck. Actually, we couldn't afford her at all, but she felt sorry for the little critter. It was no good, though; he was too good for this world and didn't last 'til spring.

"Ma come to see me one day and grabbed my dresstail and tied a knot in it before I slipped through my collar. Without howdy-do or good-bye to Ace, she carted me off home to fatten me up.

"I fiddled around with Ace for almost fifteen years; some times with him, sometimes without. When Ma took me home he scattered for eighteen months and then he come home with more wrinkles in his stomach than Nellie's apron. That time he buttered me up on both sides, and I come up with twins.

"My Pa was put out. How a man that hungry could have

two barrels to his shotgun he couldn't figure, but Ace was gone again by litterin' time, so there wasn't anything Pa could do but grit his teeth. Only thing, both the twins was born with the sign on 'em. One give up the first week. The other lasted about a month. I was a little peaked about it, but Pa said it was the best way out all around.

"Ace come 'round every now and then, but seems like he'd used up his ammunition. Either that or something sickened and died in me.

"Then one day I got news Ace had borrowed a car without askin' a feller, and rode out on the highway to meet God. I was set back for a spell, but in a few months I took to widowhood like kittens to catnip."

The dying Eliza Peebler had gone to sleep during Chili's narrative, snoring stentoriously so that the incident of Chili's final days with Ace had competition and was of little comfort to anyone except Chili, who anyway was only thinking out loud.

Introducing Sarah

Hal heard the commotion through a crack in the door and stalked out with a, "Christ in the foothills."

Thus did Chili stay on. Mrs. Morgan kept on dusting and rearranging after her, and Hal kept grumbling.

Not that Hal was an abused, indecisive man. Outside on his three-quarter section of ranch and timber land, he was the law. It was just in the women's realm that he walked softly. Nobody ever knew what Hal Morgan felt about his wife, any more than they knew what he felt about his mother-in-law. In all the years Eliza Peebler had criticized and interfered and played handmaiden to God Almighty, he never turned on her. Nobody ever saw him blowing off or raising Hell in town or taking it out on his farm hands or animals. He simply absorbed it all like a body blow in a sack of feathers.

Since anyone could remember, Eliza Peebler had been a grim-lipped, bonyfaced little woman with a sparse head of hair which she pulled tight and wore in a widow's knot on top of her head. From Sarah's infancy she had bedeviled her daughter with godliness so that by the time Sarah married Hal, she was an emotional idiot.

There was no difference in Sarah's mind between a dirty house and a dirty mind; a footprint on the linoleum floor was a sinful thought, a speck of dust was a filthy word. The act of conceiving two sons was too gross to mention and since their births, she had attempted to wash away the sin of conception with soap and hot water and fiery purges. Her house and two sons were the butt of her unreasoning compulsion.

Wayne was ten years senior to Hal Junior, and had received the brunt of his mother's guilt. Along with the ablution treatment came the hickory oil. Everything a small male creature did was an offense to God and his mother's conscience. Sarah saw him only as an extension of her original sin and a punishment from above. She passed that punishment on to Wayne.

She was antagonized by his male organs and was revolted by his interest in them. From his infancy she endeavored to keep him covered up, but the harder she tried the more curiosity Wayne expressed. His mother's guilt, of course was imprinted on the child's formative mind. A driving continuous guilt, but with it a driving all-consuming, never-ending curiosity, not only about his own body, but those of other people.

Wayne never saw his mother unclothed, but he tried; coming into his parents' bedroom unexpectedly; hiding in the bushes beside the outhouse; standing outside in the dark trying to peer under the kitchen curtains on Saturday, bath night.

Sarah Morgan discovered many of these offenses and in her fury all but tore the child apart.

With Hal Junior it was somewhat different because the younger boy met his mother's fanaticism differently. He had his father's stoicism and perhaps his unimaginativeness so that while he got into occasional trouble, it was a passing incident and a matter of indifference.

Young Hal learned to read early, and if there was a book or magazine within twenty miles he sooner or later got hold of it. A traveling library came into the Yaates once a month and the boy became its prime customer.

Nobody else in the household read anything but the Bible, and while Sarah often was uneasy and suspicious of the books and questioned Hal, the boy had learned evasion and never got caught in that trap.

His mother attempted to read one of his books two or three times, but the written word was not for her and she soon gave up out of impatience, boredom, eye ache or a crick in her back.

That was the situation in Grandma Peebler's eighty-sixth year when the old lady took to bed to nurse her aching old bones and her religious mania, and Chili came as hired girl. Had the old woman been of sound mind, she'd have ordered the slattern, mountain woman off the place.

In those last befuddled months of concentrated pain and preoccupation with mortal sin, the old lady read confession and repentance into Chili's uninhibited revelations, and recommended her to Sarah. Often she specified Chili to sit with her in her restless, sleepless hours. Chili was as strong as she was stringy and handled the little dried-up grandmother with ease and surprising gentleness, considering her rough tongue.

One night the only ease the old woman could get was to huddle up on Chili's lap in the big, creaky, old rocking-chair. Sarah was unaccountably disturbed to see her mother folded peacefully on the bosom of this woman. Hal Senior said it was, "One for the birds," and grinned broadly to see God's principal witness brought to this pass.

Sarah's revulsion was fundamental, and she was deeply troubled. Chili—irreligious, frowzy and representing with her slovenly unrestrained breasts an earthy grossness— stood for everything worldly. What shocked Sarah most was her momentary anger that it was her mother, and not she, who was clasped to Chili's bosom.

A deep basic hunger for a lap, a breast and reassuring arms about her, shook her like an ague. She thrust the thought away instantly in horror. She couldn't know this envious moment went back to her babyhood, and the aching for a gentleness and loving she didn't get from the strict Pennsylvania Dutch Eliza Peebler, had been inherited from her mother's own hidebound, religious, love-destroying family, whose tenets had been that repression and austerity were the only way to the Kingdom of God.

A Closer Look at Jack

That was the night Chili rocked the old lady until dawn and filled in some of the more lurid autobiographical details of her second marriage, including a thumbnail biography of Jack Lucey.

"Now then, Miz Peebler, you ain't comfortable, you sing out, and we'll do somethin' else with your old hide besides send it to the tannery," she said with a cheerful cackle.

The old lady's murmur indicated her mind was far from clear.

"Well, Ma'am," began Chili, "I bin thinkin' about Jack all day. Like I say, Jack died on our honeymoon, and you know the thing he regretted most? That he'd finally married a woman who wasn't hidebound in any direction, and he wasn't living to enjoy it. 'Most men,' Jack said, 'was clawed to death by a woman's good intentions.' Them was his last words except for, 'light me a cigareet, honey.'

"I'm a suck-egg mule, Miz Peebler, Ma'am, if men ain't every one of 'em got some miserable side to 'em. Ace was a wandering man; woman could never put her finger on him when she wanted him; Jack sucked up cigareets like a fire-eater at a freak show. I never seen a man bound to a filthy habit like Jack. I plumb think he killed hisself with the amount of weed he took. Like a juggler; lightin' a cigareet with one hand whilst feeling his pocket with the other. I've come into the hotel bedroom some nights on our honey-moon and thought the bedclothes was on fire."

"Resist the evil that is in men's minds," murmured Eliza Peebler from some far distant realm.

"I never did have much luck with husbands," agreed Chili. "Ace gave me three children, all with the sign on them; Jack had the sign when I married him; and sometimes I wonder if Willy ain't just too no-account to come under God's notice.

"My own Pappy come out of the Tennessee mountains, but he was a provider from 'way back. He said mountain men had a lazy reputation on account of such people as Ace. Jack was a Washington man; the Lord only knows what barren waste whelped Willy."

Go Wash Her Feet

Eliza Peebler died the following week. At the last she recovered both strength and lucidity and demanded to be set up in the rocker and wanted her feet washed. She wanted Hal Morgan to do it. Hal said he'd be Goddamned if he would, and went out to the cow barn, mad.

Old Man Starr was finished with shoveling out the manure, and he'd just put fresh hay in the mangers when his boss stomped in. The doors and windows were open, and the sun shone in, so the barn was light and airy and sweet-smelling to a country man, and Hal felt better and simmered down. But he did say to Tom, "That old woman's around my neck like a drowning kitten in a sack of rocks."

"She's a fine old lady, Mr. Morgan."

"Then maybe you'd like to go in and wash her feet."

Tom's eyes lighted up. "Praise God," he said.

Hal eyed him sourly, "What's that mean?"

"Why the Lord come in weary and dusty, and Mary and Martha made him sit down and they poured water and sweetsmelling oil in a basin and washed his feet and dried them with their hair."

"Honest to Christ," muttered Hal. He stalked to the door, then turned. "Go up to the house, see if you can help

18

Mrs. Morgan and Chili satisfy the old woman."

Old Man Starr went readily and stayed to wash Grandma Peebler's feet and pray with the old lady and sing hymns and was generally a great satisfaction to Eliza Peebler and himself.

Strange, the perversions the inhibited man will use to find release for ecstasy. All her life this old woman had taken her Saturday night bath wearing a nightgown, because it was immoral to look upon the human body unclothed. But even for a being who branded sex as abhorrent, laughter as bawdy, tears as weakness, and all joy abominable, there had to be an outlet for emotional experience. Eliza Peebler found it in a religious sect which had culled Jesus' footwashing episode from all the beauty of the New Testament. And stranger still that it was imperative the women wash the male initiates' feet and the men should wash the women's.

Grandma must have known she was close to the end and had wanted once more to expose her feet to the sight of a man; "Worshipping the Lord in abject humility," Old Tom called it. That was on a Wednesday, and that night Eliza Peebler died in her sleep.

The morning after Eliza Peebler died, Old Man Starr came to the kitchen door to pay respects and an offer to pray with the family and ask God's comfort. Hal Senior told him to go back to his chores; that he might be the personal representative of Grandma's God in-between times, but from dawn to dark he was a hired hand. Hal probably wouldn't have been so short except that he was so all-fired relieved that the saddle girth finally had been unfastened, and it felt so good that he couldn't bear any sanctimony cluttering up the premises.

Tom Starr was more aggrieved than angered, and when Hal rode off to the P&X Mill to have a casket knocked together, he went back. Sarah answered. When he repeated his offer, a spasm of hatred and revulsion crossed her face, and she shut the door violently. It was an unaccountable act. She had always liked Tom and now to hate the sight of his benign patriarchal visage made no sense to her; unconscious of the roots of resentments against her mother's grim, barren austerity, buried forty-five years deep from childhood. She had always supposed she loved the old lady. Now her true emotions leapt out, unleashed against the one person who professed the same unctuous, sterile grimness.

Her violence did her one kindness. It brought on the only tears Sarah shed. They came in a gush of emotion as painful and relieving as a first erotic emission.

Chili half walked, half carried the distraught woman into her bedroom and administered with a native sympathy and gentleness that opened new floodgates.

Sarah the woman, uncontrollably became Sarah the child; the frightened, bewildered waif in a grim repellent world whose every happy impulse had been quenched by staring, disapproving eyes of grim-faced elders who did not laugh and whose only smiles were derisive or maliciously mocking.

The old Chinese bound their girls' feet to distort them, but this Pennsylvania Dutch family into which Sarah was born, bound its daughters' souls with insane fear of everlasting torment; bound their hands against any impulsive self-expression; warped the creative impulse and instinctive call to beauty and nature into a grotesque monster who lay chained below the surface.

This hideous creature so effectively bound, took vengeance by eating out all sweetness, all light and all hope. It ravaged her into a caricature of her own mother. The old lady had iron in her soul. If there had ever been iron in Sarah, it had been eaten by the rust of guilt, fear and self-loathing.

"I was not a Christian girl," she wept in Chili's arms. "When there was dancing, I wanted to dance. Once I stood outside a house where music was playing, and I could hear laughter inside and I reviled God that I wasn't inside. I stood for an hour in a driving rain listening and hating, sick with something I could only feel. I came home with chills and fever and two days later nearly died with pneumonia.

"My father was as stern as my mother. He spoke always in anger, and his hand was heavy. When he turned it against us children, it wasn't a slap, it was a blow. It always came unexpectedly, which was more hatefully unjust than the cuffing. My ears still ring, and sometimes I can barely restrain myself.

"Mother never slapped us, but then she never kissed us either."

Chili bent and kissed the weeping woman, and Sarah Morgan clung to her convulsively.

The unburdening went on hour after hour; the bitterness; the slipping away of her brother and sisters; the untimely and unregretted passing of her father; the inability or perhaps unwillingness to disassociate herself from her mother; her unaccountable marriage to Hal, whom she never knew or tried to know and who was an unwelcome stranger in her bed, bringing two more strangers into her life in the persons of her sons, Wayne and Hal Junior.

Almost everything she unburdened led up to sex, but each time it ended just short of the subject itself. Even in her travail, the monster remained chained and unapproachable. In the end she fell into an exhausted sleep.

She awoke controlled, dry-eyed, master of herself and never again referred to those hours of agony. But from that day Chili was as much a fixture in the Morgan house as the wood stove in the kitchen.

Chili with her loose mouth had always been a gossipy woman whose dresstails never touched her bottom until all the neighbors had heard, but she didn't talk about her mistress to anyone, except the one comment to Willy, "The skunks littered under her Pappy's cabin early, and the poor thing soured on the cob."

PART II

Strangers in Yaates Valley

"When it comes to the kitchen work," Romeo McFeddor avows, "Chili Winneger is a six-pronged windmill a-fightin' fire on three fronts. I never *did* see a female with so many hands at supper time. The way she c'n peel spuds, stir cornbread, draw a grouse, gut trout, stoke wood in the firebox, and still find time to scratch an itch between her shoulder blades, I swear by McGrudder's six virtuous taws that sometimes I think that Ozarkian woman's got a extra pair of arms where other females wear their pretties."

The upper sector of Yaates Valley, Montana, is lavish with partridge, grouse and quail in mid-fall before the first snows, what with the temperature down to near zero and the crimping frost making picture postcards out of the high mountain meadows. That is the time of year the Morgan hay ranch is turned into a rough and ready guest ranch for a few select Seattle and Spokane game-bird hunters. The harvest is in and the casual hay-hands long gone, so the bunkhouse, a couple of log cabins and the spare bedrooms in the main house are turned into guest quarters. Six visitors at a time are all Morgan will accommodate, with seldom any women. Wilderness Montana, with its outdoor plumbing, creek water carried to the cabins in buckets, and a metal washtub and a pail of hot water from the back of the kitchen stove for bathing, is too primitive for the average city wife.

23

Now that Grandma Peebler's fragile mind and body had wandered off to "Paradise Enow," as Old Man Starr put it, just prior to this fall's hunting season, Hal Morgan had kept Chili on to cook and mind for the guests and had inveigled the reluctant Romeo McFeddor, Chili's occasional boyfriend, into helping her with the guest cabins and bunkhouse work, and to help Old Man Starr milk the thirty head of Guernseys and handle the riding horses.

The first time Morgan asked Romeo to help with the guests, he snorted, "I'd ruther be in hell with my back broke. If I was *that* empty I'd put on a pair of bat wings and snap for gnats."

The next time Morgan asked him, he complained, "A man that was born, bred, and buttered in the high hills just plain can't stomach furriners. My gorge rises before the howdies is over. I know, I've tried it."

Then on Sunday, Chili flounced by him at the Upper Fork on her way to church, and Romeo fell in beside her and wanted to know if she was ruffling her feathers at him or whether she was just throwin' rocks at Creation.

"Man named Romeo McFeddor stirs my hackles something ridick'lus," Chili snapped. Romeo looked surprised and pained, but kept silent. He had to, because Chili's tongue was loose at both ends. "My better sense told me, don't *ever* look to anybody named McFeddor for *nothing*. He'll stand at the Pearly Gates and misguide infant souls on the road to Hell, given the chance."

Romeo rolled the cud of crimp cut, spat generously and effectively, and grinned. "I'd thought some of takin' you to the annual Melvin Stump Ranch fracas a week from Saturday night, but now it looks like you'd rather go with Willy."

Chili tossed her head. "Oh, Willy'll be there, don't

never worry about that!" Willy was Chili's third husband, though, as Chili said, you'd hardly know it, except both their last names was Winneger. "Yep," she repeated, "Willy'll be there—down on his hands and knees lookin' for a corner to rest in."

"Accordin' to rumors," Romeo said, "that Willy likes it best up on the Ridge where both the corn and the girls are twice twisted."

"And I don't suppose," Chili said pointedly, "that the rumor has come to your ears yet that I'm still up at Hal Morgan's layout for the game-bird shootin'?"

Romeo nodded. "I heard."

"Then naturally you know I'm up there alone and forlorn, and Willy is away up on the Ridge wastin' hisself! So what do you do?"

Romeo opened his mouth, but Chili beat him to it. "So you tell Hal Morgan you won't touch his job of work with a ten-foot pole, but what you're really sayin' is that you won't touch Chili Winneger with a ten-foot pole."

"Chili," protested Romeo ardently, "if I had a ten-foot pole. ..." He broke off and shook his head. "No," he said regretfully, "that wouldn't be practical." Then he reached up, took off his big, misused hat and slapped it on his thigh enthusiastically, "By St. Nick's Forked Tail," he cried, "I'm a-gonna *take* Hal Morgan's job! I'll bring along my sougans and I'll spread 'em out in the haymow and. ..." He shook his head and grinned broadly at the bridling Chili. "What you s'pose Hal'll say if he finds out a old buzzard like me has built a love nest in his barn? Just natcherly raise hell, I misdoubt."

They had come to the steps of the little white community church. Chili took his arm encouragingly, but Romeo shied and backed away. "I don't do no galin' nor frolickin' in no house of the hypocrites," he said.

Chili waggled her behind mounting the steps and was received into the bosom of the church by the Reverend Mr. Grocer, who would cover fifty miles and two more churches this day, after the Yaates Valley services.

Steeped in Naughtiness

On Romeo's third day at the ranch, when young Fred Crowle and Jewels Laraby stumbled in on trail-weary horses from a long and unsuccessful expedition without a bird between them, Jewels was too tired to be very upset, but Fred was in a foul temper. The other guests besides Laraby at the ranch this week were James Thomas, Seattle attorney; his exceptionally lovely daughter, Ann, in her early twenties; and young Crowle, a junior member of the law firm. Obviously Ann was the apple of her father's eye, and just as obviously there was at least an understanding between Ann and Fred.

But this night Fred was in a furious temper, and when they dismounted from their horses he threw the reins into Romeo's face and exclaimed, "What the devil kind of hunting country is this?" Romeo's eyes flickered, but he kept his face stolid, squirted tobacco juice on the ground a neat two inches from Fred's boot, and without a word turned to take Jewels horse, but Fred pulled him around. "Are you turning your back on me?" he challenged.

Romeo stared at young Crowle for a long moment and then said in a soft drawl, "Don't *never* do that again. Don't grab a man's arm 'les you aim to tear it off and beat him to death with the bloody stump." Then in a normal voice he announced casually that after supper he would not be available inasmuch as he was going down to the Melvin Stump Ranch for a barn dance.

The contrast of Romeo's anticipated pleasure against his own frustrating day roused an ill-humored perversity in Fred. He looked at Laraby. "How would you like to go to a shirttail barn dance tonight?"

Before Jewels could deny any such desire, Fred looked into Romeo's stony face with a blustering authority and demanded, "How about it, McFeddor? You'd like to take us, wouldn't you?"

After a split-second, the chill faded from Romeo's eyes and a sardonic grin twisted his face.

"What kind of citizens do you have at these Yaates dances?" Fred persisted.

Romeo shrugged. "What ain't mis-begot or mis-created are ill-conditioned somethin' scandalous."

"Friends of yours, aren't they?" Fred asked suspiciously.

Romeo looked indignant.

"Well, aren't they?"

"I never said so."

Romeo's reluctant answers were beginning to intrigue Fred. "Come on, open up," he persisted. "What are the girls like?"

Romeo thought young Crowle's interest strange, considering there was a girl up at the house as pretty as Ann, and especially as she was the daughter of his boss. But Crowle was as cross as two sticks and in a contrary mood. "The girls! The girls!" His eyes were on Romeo eagerly. "What are they like?"

"They got two legs apiece."

Fred's eyes sparkled. "You've seen them then?"

"They ain't worth a second look."

"Oh?" Young Crowle's face fell. He looked like a disappointed baby.

Suddenly Romeo's face relaxed in humorous conspiracy. "Unless maybe you're thinking of Molly Hester. She's got two of the most infamous legs to ever make a man's saliva glands water."

Laraby was watching Romeo and he could see, as plain as day, that Romeo was saying to himself, "If that young squirt of an outlander is a-lookin for trouble, then why not give it to him."

Fred was hooked. "Tell us about Molly."

Romeo pretended to hedge. "A man don't talk about the neighbor girls," he said virtuously, then added gratuitously, "However, that there Molly is hell-born fodder for a man with a big appetite."

Fred grinned, gave Romeo a knowing wink, and took his arm, man to man. "Will she be at the dance tonight?"

Romeo hated to be touched, but he held still. "She never misses."

"And she's an appetizing dish? That what you're saying?" Fred squeezed Romeo's arm to show his appreciation.

Romeo moved a restless foot and then stood still. "Rinsed in shortcomings and ironed crooked," he promised the younger man solemnly.

"She's not married, is she?" Fred asked with sudden sternness. "How old is she?"

Romeo shrugged. "Well, she got lost to virtue and out-of-plumb when she was maybe fifteen. That was three, four summers ago."

"And she's not married?"

"Well, she sure *ought* to be, but she ain't. Molly slipped into sin like Sadie in Satin."

"And good-looking?" Fred asked for reassurance.

Romeo confirmed it. "A lavish of pretties and past prayin' for seven miles back." He nodded encouragingly and then added, virtue heavy in his voice, "Not that I'd ever mis-say anything agin Molly. She's nice folks! Jes' that she got steeped in naughtiness early and dried crooked on the line."

Jewels already knew about Molly Hester from Hal Morgan, and Romeo might have added that Molly recently had been taken into the cabin of a two-hundred-twenty-pound P&X Mills sawyer named Jim Tate, who was so jealous of Molly he was either going to kill her or somebody else before spring.

Lie Down Man, You're Dead

Up in the Yaates Valley country it was deep fall, just before the big snows, but with the cold playing footsie with zero, and frosty mornings white, crisp and clear. In the Morgan kitchen it was drawing on towards evening. Under the bedazzling Coleman lantern, Chili Winneger was building supper for the game-bird hunters.

Leaning against the door frame, Ann Thomas, the only female guest and daughter of the Seattle attorney, silently watched the raw-boned, slattern hill-woman with affectionate amusement. It was a sight the way Chili shoved stick wood into the firebox of the stove like "Satan castin' sinners"; the way she slip-slapped dirty utensils into the big dishpan heating on the back of the stove; the easy way she slashed open and cleaned trout, like she was kin to 'em; the way she hummed "I'd Rather Marry a Rich Man" through her nose as she clattered the skillets; and flung down a can of bear grease for frying, her unhampered pendulous breasts working under her apron like mama and papa beavers with winter coming on.

When Chili turned to the hand pump at the sink, she became aware of the invasion in her kitchen. She already had grown generously fond of her young guest; it was lonely up here in the backcountry, being the only member of her sex, and Ann Thomas was a good listener.

"Land a-goshen, child, how long you been a-standin' there?"

Ann smiled and walked over to the stove. A deep mischievous dimple appeared in her young, smooth cheek. "I've been watching you and Romeo McFeddor. I think he likes you." She kept her eyes on the venison chops spluttering in their skillet of bear fat.

Chili gave the girl a sharp glance. "I'm a married woman," she said finally, by way of explaining nothing.

"Oh, I didn't know that." The faint pink of embarrassment flushed the girl's cheeks.

"Yep! Been married to Willy seven years; my third and biggest mistake." Chili poured cornbread batter into two oblong baking pans and shoved them in the oven.

"I don't think Romeo likes me." Ann frowned, puzzled.

"Yaaters is most all cantankerous critters with Outlanders. Specially pretty, blonde-headed ones that're way out of reach."

Ann's eyes opened wide. "Why, Romeo's older than my father!"

Chili cackled.

Ann insisted, "You mean he's interested in girls at his age?"

"I don't know about your city slickers," Chili said goodhumoredly, "but mountain men is interested in women up to the minute the good Lord says "Lie down man, you're dead!""

Ann laughed, sobered, and said curiously, "Tell me about your husband."

"Willy? Why, Willy's broad as daylight and low down to

the ground. Comes from fatty degeneration of his irresistance to mountain liquor, huckleberry cobbler, and fence-corner daisies."

"I don't think I've seen him, have I?" Ann hung onto her amusement.

Chili shrugged. "He's mostly up on the Ridge where the whiskey is cheap and the women's plentiful."

Ann was shocked. "You mean you *know* he sees other women?"

Chili snorted and said "Ha!" The two expressions put together came out in the form of a big juicy raspberry.

"And you're not jealous?"

"Willy's had a miserable row all his life," Chili said defensively. "Everybody's allowed some rewards for clingin' to the rope of life when all you got to do is let loose and drop down into the chasm for ever and ever."

Ann stared, but Chili was too busy to notice.

"I've heard his ma tell how folks said the sign was on Willy from his first-born suckle day, and she'd never raise him. But she did, defects and all. I hear tell he was a mangy little sprout. More colds than Newcastle; faucety-nosed and no handkerchief; tonsillectomy every winter and adenoids as big as mountain oysters; ears and knuckles that chapped in the frost like raw meat. A vomity little poot; put him in a spring buggy for a Sunday drive to church and two minutes later everybody had to turn back and change clothes and fumigate."

"Poor little Willy!" Ann's voice was sympathetic, but there were dancing lights of laughter in her eyes.

Chili looked at her and said cheerfully, "Worst was his weak gum-bones. A travelin' dentist said he'd be a teether all his life, so they had 'em all pulled out when Willy was ten."

"Oh no!" Ann protested.

Chili nodded, picking up the big skillet of cottage fries, and with a twist of the wrist flipped the whole lot, brown side up. "His papa made him false teeth out of a piece of old inner tube, some baling wire, and a handful of bear teeth. Inside of three months Willy could tear meat with the best of 'em. He really took to his serious drinking, howsomever, when he got a corny disposition of the feet."

"Got what?" Ann giggled despite herself.

"It's a fact!" Chili swore solemnly, beginning to drop the trout in the big spider of hot grease. "That man can grow more corn on his feet than Old Nick's got oats. It turned Willy agin't anything you can't do sittin' or layin', and up here in the Yaates they ain't much a man can do sittin' or layin' that'd make him what you'd call a good provider."

"And you think that justifies his drinking and running after girls?" Ann persisted dubiously.

"He ain't much as husbands go," Chili agreed cheerfully. "But then show me a man who is."

"Men," she said, "are as alike as split rails. Some warped a mite one way, some another; knotty in different places, but all hewed rough—befogged, botched, and splintery."

"I don't believe it," Ann stated defensively, her pretty cheeks flushing.

"Miss Ann, honey, where you been raised? Why, child, every mountain girl learns about men whilst still a-sucklin'. It comes in the milk along with all the other goodies."

Suddenly Chili was twice as busy. "Now, then, honey, go powder your nose. Supper's about on!"

As Ann went out the kitchen door, Chili slid the chops out of the frying pans onto an oblong platter and put them at the back of the range; took out the cornbread, now creamy gold and crisp; slid the cottage fries onto another platter out of the warming oven, and then began lifting the crisp, tender white-fleshed trout from the spider.

"Such an innocent young thing," Chili muttered to herself. "And just let me catch McFeddor a-makin' eyes in my direction in front of that child. I'll tear out his wicked disposition and make him eat it right there."

Old Nick's Pen Wiper

When Seattle attorney, James Thomas, and his daughter, Ann, sat down with the rest of Hal Morgan's game-bird hunters at the big guest table just off the kitchen, Chili Winneger stormed in with an armful of victuals, set them down and then stormed out for more. It was as she was coming through the swinging door the second time that Fred Crowle, the junior in Thomas' legal firm and a possible contestant for Ann's hand, lit the fire under the powder keg.

All he said was, "Romeo McFeddor has been telling me about the barn dance at the Melvin Stump Ranch tonight and I thought I'd like to go." It was easy to tell by the look in his eyes that the cold and isolation up here in the Yaates Valley primitive area were making Fred itch with anticipation. Ann caught fire immediately. She also had an itch for adventure, but her need was more of the emotional than the physical, while Fred's urge, fed by Romeo at the trough of innuendo and insinuation, was pronounced, insistent and very much localized. Romeo had made it quite plain what went on at a Yaates Valley barn dance.

Mr. Thomas was doubtful. "Outside hunters, back up in this country, are here on sufferance. . . ." He broke off as Chili slammed down a plate of corn bread and he caught her look of angry disapproval. "What is your opinion, Chili? What do you think about it?"

"I think I'll go out and shoot Romeo McFeddor dead in his tracks," she announced with a vicious flounce.

"McFeddor's pawin' the good earth for trouble. He'd be pleased as a skunk in a churn should you go down to the Melvin Stump Ranch and start a ruckus."

"Well, that settles *that!*" Mr. Thomas looked at Ann's disappointment and young Crowle's scowl of discontent. "We had this out at the county seat with the sheriff when we got our hunting permits," the older lawyer pointed out. "At the time he said we were foolish to come up here where we are not wanted. He also said at the first sign of trouble, out we go."

Chili had been standing behind Ann, hands on hips, listening with approval. She waited with suspenseful watchfulness for Fred's reply.

It took him a long moment to swallow his regret. "Forget it," he muttered, "I'm dog-tired anyway."

Ann looked up over her shoulder at Chili, chagrined. "Why shouldn't we go? We'd love it."

"No, you wouldn't, honey," Chili said decisively. "It just ain't no place for nice folks."

"Then why did Romeo mention it?" Fred countered resentfully.

"That McFeddor's the illest critter this side of Hell Creek. I'm almighty bored at you folks a-bein' took in by him. He's be-rift!"

"Ill?"

Chili nodded. "Mean as his hide'll hold. He's got so much meanness he keeps it in a pot under his bed and still has two bales in the barn." Chili nodded emphatically. "There's a narrowminded man that'd rather get a furriner into trouble than eat Sunday pie."

After supper Ann went listlessly into the living room to sit beside the open fire. Fred was drawn to the barns where Romeo was finishing his chores. A single glance and Romeo knew he had seeded stormy weather.

"Goin' down to the Melvin barn dance?" he asked, pitching a forkfull of sweetsmelling mountain meadow hay into a boxstall manger.

"How far is it?" Fred asked glumly.

"Less than six miles. You can't miss it! Barn'll be lit up to shame Christmas. Barnyard'll be full of wagons and horses and a spit of automobiles."

"Chili says Outlanders don't belong down there."

Romeo leaned on his pitchfork and bit off a cud from his frayed plug, then said thoughtfully, "Females sure are funny critters."

Fred waited.

Romeo nodded. "Chili prob'ly was a-figgerin' on soapin' herself good tonight. Wouldn't want her people up here to see her cavortin', most likely."

"Is that why she was so angry? Because we'd make her self-conscious and spoil her good time?"

"Howsomever," Romeo pondered soberly, "should you come in kinda late, after she's had a couple of belts of Max Shoemaker's mountain brew, she'll prob'ly fall on your neck like a long lost sister."

"I guess no one is going." Fred turned reluctantly away and headed for the door.

"Should you decide different, look me up. Proud to

lead you to the trough. It'll be a restless night, most likely. They'll be samplin' a-plenty, liquor and otherwise."

Fred hesitated, then called back, "You say Molly Hester'll be there?"

"Bound to be, Mr. Crowle! Bound to be!"

Fred stepped out into the night air. It wasn't eight o'clock yet, but already the thermometer was down to the first level and still sinking. The crisp, cold air tingled on his flushed cheeks and penetrated his clothing, caressing his over-sensitive skin with small impertinent, icy fingers.

"Uh-huh, Molly'd be there." Romeo would have done young Crowle a mighty big service had he said big Jim Tate, the P&X sawyer, also would be there watching Molly every minute. Tate was an acknowledged rascal in his own right, a man without excuse or hope at any time, a blot on the name of Yaates Valley as big as Old Nick's pen wiper when he was drunk; and he was always drunk at a barn dance.

Romeo's Three Silver Legs

It was a week after the Melvin Stump Ranch barn dance and minor massacre up in the Yaates Valley in northern Montana that Romeo McFeddor was sitting on the bunkhouse porch steps chewing on a straw and meditating with sheer animal gusto over all the devilment he'd brought to pass in the last few days.

For instance, Yaates Valley was shet of all outlander game-bird hunters, including Lawyer Thomas, his yaller-haired daughter, Ann, and Fred Crowle, who had arrived as Ann's young man and who had departed an excommunicated disgrace. Romeo recalled with unmixed pleasure how he had stirred young Crowle's red blood with talk of Molly Hester, who had been rompin' through the thorn patch since she was fifteen and was still not only the willingest, but the plumpest and prettiest partridge in the whole of Yaates Valley.

"Hey-y-y, you, McFeddor!"

Romeo leaped three feet and come down, splitting the stepboard under his tailbone.

"I thought so; guilty conscience!"

"By God, woman! Creepin' up on a man and yellin' down his earpipes!"

"You sowed your crop of meanness last week down at

the Melvin Stump Ranch, and now you sit there, happy as a kitty in catnip. Shame should be bustin' out all over you in great ugly blotches, but I Swear to Who Laid the Chunk, you've got such a calloused hide, you don't even look sorry." Chili Winneger, long, gangling, with arms like a windmill's, feet apart, stood rocking back and forth on heel and toe. "You tempted that gander-eyed Crowle boy with that fencecorner seedlin', Molly Hester, and knowin' all the time she was holin' up for the winter with that P&X sawyer, Jim Tate."

"I only told him what he wanted to know."

"You tempted him 'til he could taste her six miles off, and him engaged to that nice, sheltered Miss Ann Thomas."

Romeo smirked. "I wouldn't exactly say nice and sheltered after what I seen at the Melvin Stump Ranch."

"And there's some *more* worms that'll be eatin' your everlastin' soul for ever and ever more."

"T'weren't *my* fault, when Fred got out the car to go down to the dance lookin' for Molly, that the yaller-haired city minx sneaked in the back and went along."

"You tempted the boy. . ."

"Hell, woman, temptations is with you every minute of every day like fleas on Rover. And I didn't give Fred Crowle the itch! If I tried to help him to scratch it, so much for me! It's what any good samaritan would do."

Chili snorted. "You tempted the boy, and Miss Ann went along to protect her interests, and the whole blame is on you."

"Why did this Ann character have to *hide* in the back of the car?" Romeo demanded.

"Because Fred wouldn't have took her."

"Well, at least why didn't she let Fred know after they'd arrived at the Melvin Place?" And then without waiting to be answered, Romeo went on virtuously, "She went for the same reason Fred went. Her dresstail was on fire and she went to get the flames put out."

"If you got any brains at all, McFeddor," Chili said haughtily, "they wouldn't show under a magnifying glass. When young Crowle started out the door with Molly, Jim Tate was right behind breathin' murder down his neck until Miss Ann stepped up close to Jim, put her arms around his neck and kissed him square on the mouth."

"I seen it," chortled Romeo. "She jes' kinda melted into his arms. A real fence-corner peach. Another Molly Hester under the skin."

"I swear, McFeddor," Chili raged, "if you was the only man on earth and you had three silver legs, I still would prefer to die a harmless, untouched maiden. Miss Ann didn't go after that drunken sawyer for any other reason but to get his mind off of Molly and Fred."

"Which she did do," Romeo nodded appreciatively. "Which she did do."

"She saved Fred Crowle's life," Chili protested indignantly. "And then what does that poor fool of a boy do? Why, he catches Miss Ann in the sawyer's drunken clutches and hits him over the head with a fence rail. It's just lucky Tate was both drunk and stunned, or Fred Crowle would have been strangled to death with his own entrails."

"Especially," chuckled Romeo, "when Molly and her clan wanted to get in on the fun. I don't know how you got Fred back in the car. Molly and her sisters were a-rippin' our city-gal plumb to the rind. They had her down to the last layer when I pulled her free and dumped her in beside Fred."

Chili glowered. "And now they ain't a single outlander bird hunter left in the whole Yaates Valley, and Hal Morgan's closin' up and that means you and me ain't got no more jobs than grasshoppers."

Romeo eyed the forty-five-year-old, scrawny Ozarkian woman with interest. "Willy's up on the Ridge where the whiskey's free and the wimmen easy. Willy's shack'll be a mite lonesome. How about comin' down to my cabin and cook for me?"

"You remind me of the time the skunks littered under our house." Chili flounced off, and Romeo leaned back easy like. Well, she didn't say no, did she?

PART III

Old Man Starr

July, 1939

It was one of those everlasting days in July when Old Man Starr, "tree high, stone solid, and water pure," in Yaates vernacular, came striding up the Forest Service road, his white hair shining under the filtered sun, and whiter beard flowing in the warm fitful summer breeze.

He was indeed a tall straight stem of a man, gaunt with sixty-five seasons of wind and weather. Spare he was, still a granite wall of a figure with all the loose sand eroded out of the crevices. His face shone with the placid simplicity of a glacial lake, and to the blue afternoon sky he sang lustily, "Praise God from whom all blessings flow."

Between the lines he broke off with explosive ejaculations of, "Praise the Lord!" and "God be praised. Praise Him all creatures here below."

Old Man Starr was an ambulatory one-man revival meeting; hymns, worship, prayer, confessed sinner, repentant and saved, all rolled into one. Under his arm he carried a Bible. He was a man to stand up and be counted. In his relentless zeal he was the Rev. Mr. Grocer's most ardent and ofttimes most difficult parishioner. He wore his religion as "bright flying banners." Both the white banner of purity, and

45

the warrior's red banner of aggression against sin. Not only Yaates Valley *sin*. Sin at the mill, the mine, the logging camps, the county seat seventy miles away, and on the Ridge where Original Sin was invented and flourished among the "Sodomites and the Gomorrahites." The quotes are Old Man Starr's!

"Praise Him above all ye heavenly hosts!"

It was Sunday, and the old man was returning home to Hal Morgan's ranch where he was a dairy hand. He was wonderful with cows. Hal Senior said he'd seen him take a young heifer troubled with her first calving and bring her through with a gentleness that sure was tender to see. Old Man Starr said anyone could do it.

"First you pray to God to steady your hand, then you watch the rhythm, and at the right moment grab a-holt and heave. A calf's got to be born front feet first. Ninety-nine times out of a hundred, if a cow has trouble it's because the Devil's crawled inside and fouled up a front leg.

Every mischance in Nature is the work of Tom Starr's and God Almighty's personal archenemy, the Devil; and a very real devil Starr made him out to be, standing foursquare against his Satanic tomfoolery.

"Praise Father, Son, and Holy Ghost."

His voice was full, throaty, and resonant, echoing and re-echoing down the corridor of giant fir and Tamaracks lining the roadway between the meeting house where Services had just ended, and Seth Bascomb's cabin, known as the Federal Building on Friday mail day, where Romeo McFeddor sat whittling and expectorating.

This was the third Sunday of the month, the Rev. Mr. Grocer's morning to preach in Yaates Valley on his circuit of country churches, and Seth's monthly church day.

Romeo never went near the meeting house, Rev. Mr. Grocer or no Reverend, and so had forgot Seth wouldn't be home. In fact, he'd forgot it was Sunday until he heard Old Man Starr's voice booming up the road ahead of him.

Comfortable on the steps, his backside to the warming sunshine, Romeo listened a moment, then spitting a loose-goose stream of tobacco juice disdainfully, paid no more heed.

"Praise the Lord," hailed the old man, catching sight of McFeddor. "God's in his Heaven, Mr. McFeddor."

"Well, tell him to stay there," Romeo said sourly.

"Blasphemy!" rebuked Tom coming to a standstill before the steps.

Romeo eyed him with humorous contempt. "Well, if you ain't greased, galloused and glossed over."

"I've been to meet my Lord," the old man said with dignity.

"What'd he have to say for hisself?"

"All's well with the world," Tom responded benignly.

"You mean He ain't heard about the Bates girl bein' in a family way again?"

"The sins of the fathers," cried Old Man Starr, his patriarchal beard quivering.

"Wasn't her father," said Romeo, "it was one of the new boys up at the P&X Mill."

"God will strike him dead!"

"Well, he hain't up to now," commented Romeo optimistically, "and the way I heard it, she asked for it. Think God might like the facts?"

"If it will relieve you to unburden your soul."

"Well, according to folks, Susie Bates is telling the story on herself. 'My claws was a-itching in their sheath, and my back hair was arching, and then along came *him*; and I was a cooked goose!' And he sure left an impression; she's full as a cream jug."

"She will be a better girl for having cleansed her soul by confession," Starr said piously.

"Knowing Susie, her Ma asked her if she was sure it was the P&X Mill boy. Susie said, 'Well, he was a bigger man to start; seems reasonable he must have left a part of him lodged there.'"

"He going to marry her?" The old man looked at Romeo accusingly.

"Susie's gonna make a try for it. Else why would she have named him?"

"The Lord will see to it."

Romeo grinned, "The Lord sure took care of Susie the last time, or maybe it was her own idea jumping off high places until she broke her basket of eggs."

"The whole Bates family is a thorn in the side of our Lord."

Romeo shrugged, "Well, when you catch a varmit in your trap, you either dispose of it or fix to live with it."

"Thou shalt not commit murder!"

"The Lord giveth and the Lord takes away," Romeo countered.

Old Man Starr's moist blue eyes scorched Romeo who was whittling and didn't notice.

"All men are evil, and all women are weak vessels," Tom said in a vibrant voice.

"Fence-corner peaches are sweetest," Romeo countered and added, "Girl comes along like Susie, nipple high, perfumed and giddy as a spiral gust, what's a man going to do?"

"Tuberose sweet and cabbage rotten," Old Man Starr said gloomily.

"Sit down a spell," Romeo invited.

The old man didn't deign to answer. He turned back onto the forest road to where it branched off upwards to Grizzly Flats and the Morgan ranch. It was a long five miles mostly on the rise, but Tom Starr walked it with ease and pleasure. He thought some about the Rev. Mr. Grocer's sermon, wishing this servant of God breathed more brimstone. He quoted scripture to every creature in earshot:

"I lift mine eyes to the hills from whence cometh my strength."

He thought with regretful indignation of Susie and the P&X boy and prayed aloud that God would bring them to repentance and marriage.

The old man's eyes were not entirely turned inward. He enjoyed the grandeur of this Montana wild country which spread to the horizon as the road rose out of the big timber. Smoky blue foothills rimmed the distant foreground across a vastness of coyote, buck brush and stands of Lodgepole pines. Behind them the sawtooth snow peaks of the

Canadian Rockies jutted skyward like an airy circle of frosty crags and castles.

Quail and grouse and brush rabbits skittered in the high weeds; all the little varmits in the wind and grass were a-humming and squeaking and piping, and angels and cat squirrels peeped out to smile from every glory hole.

Old Man Starr was in his element at milking time, with seventeen fawn-and-white Jersey cows lined up in their stanchions, switching flies and munching the sweet hay, their deerlike ears alert to the slightest move behind them. The cheerful clink of the pail, the businesslike scrape of the three-legged milking stool, the solid rumble of milk through the strainer pouring into the ten-gallon cans were as much a part of the familiar evening symphony as Tom's vocalizing.

The Jersey cow was on the skittish side, but under the ministration of the old man's practiced hands and the soothing sound of his hymns, she gave milk copiously. Sometimes he intoned scripture to the rhythm of the milk. "Blessed are the meek for they shall inherit the earth. Blessed are the pure for they shall see God."

But tonight he was singing, "I walked in the garden alone; the dew was still on the roses."

And while he sang, he was thinking of the terrible sins of the flesh that Yaaters were heir to, and what he, Tom, as the strong right arm of the Almighty should personally do about it. This problem had haunted him for years, but the preacher had said it again this morning.

"Each one of us is personally responsible," the Rev. Mr. Grocer had admonished his congregation. "I am my brother's keeper, which the Good Book says in plain words, and if I do not abide by this I am as guilty of omission as my erring brothers who wantonly commit evil."

Unconsciously Tom's song changed from the gentle abiding melody to the militant.

"Onward Christian Soldiers, marching as to war, with the Cross of Jesus, going on before."

Put It Away!

In the gathering evening dusk, pulsating and luminous as a great lustrous pearl, Hal Morgan's elder son Wayne, boneweary and sweatstained, rode in from the long afternoon of haying astride one of the work horses. He heard Old Man Starr's rich, booming voice above the rattling of harness chains and distant bawling calves in the barnyard, and his dark brooding face lightened. Of all mankind Tom was the one satisfyingly compatible fellow being.

The old man already was a fixture on the Morgan place when Wayne was born, and Wayne had turned to him early as a kind, sympathetic, tough, eccentric mentor. As he grew and strange forces took hold of him he came more and more under Tom's influence and Tom's religious exaltation.

There was something morbidly fascinating; yes, and comforting as it was unsettling, in the old man's convictions of a vengeful God who tore asunder whomsoever would mock and revile him. Tom's word pictures of hell and damnation with its eternal fires torturing unrepentant souls, filled Wayne with nameless qualms, but at the same time satisfied a strange misgiving; something in the way a sound spanking relieves a guilty child and renews his faith.

The haying season was short in the Yaate's far northern climate, so from necessity, once begun, was continuous seven days a week from daylight to dark. Thus a Sunday workday was no unusual event in July. Of all the hired hands, only Tom Starr had been available for church services,

52

as his only concern was the dairy herd.

Until last summer Wayne had helped with the milking, but after he lost the first joint of his right thumb, that hand had never been able to hold a teat properly. However, he was efficient with an axe, shovel, mattock, or canthook, and a pitchfork handle fitted into the mutilated hand as though tooled for it.

The accident had occurred the previous haying season while his ten-year-old brother, Hal Jr., had been driving the derrick horse for the Jackson Fork. Wayne was on a fresh wagonload of hay, adjusting the four-pronged fork for the twenty-foot pull up the face of the barn to the haymow. Young Hal was slumped on the back of the horse, his nose in a mutilated traveling-library book as usual, when Wayne yelled for more slack on the cable.

Young Hal heard it as a signal to start his horse. Wayne's thumb was caught and he was carried along with the empty Jackson Fork almost the whole twenty feet into the air before the runningline and pulleywheel sawed through the joint and gristle and let him fall back. Fortunately, the hay was deep and soft, but his severed thumb was squirting blood like a beheaded chicken.

Hal Sr. in his aggravated excitement took time to tan the younger boy's britches while Mrs. Morgan and Tom Starr fixed a tourniquet for Wayne. Then Morgan and Wayne drove eighty rugged miles over the upper pass to Kalispell for medical attention.

Loss of the thumb came to have a significant meaning for Wayne; also for Old Man Starr. Tom maintained it was the will of God, and Wayne believed him.

"If an eye offendeth God, pluck it out; if your tongue giveth offense, tear it out! Son, that thumb was somehow an offense unto the Almighty, so good riddance and the Lord bless you." After a brooding moment he added a footnote.

"Eyes and tongues the Bible says, but there's an over-weaning number of mighty offensive hoe-handles in this Yaates country that God would be pleased to see chopped off."

Old Man Starr's never ending pride in the Morgan family's moral leadership in the community was another subject that held Wayne unaccountably. Tom remembered Wayne's maternal grandmother as the fountainhead of family chastity and religious convictions.

"She walked with God and stood no foolishness," he would say. "It was by way of her that I got such a tight grip on the Lord! Why that old lady was so modest, she took her Saturday night bath in her nightgown and made no bones about it. She figured the human body was God's Temple, and was not meant for human eyes. And I'm proud to say your own Ma always has showed the same decency in bringing up you boys."

Tom never talked about his grandmother that Wayne didn't have at least one nightmare afterwards.

"You was an awful little ripper," the old man would say to Wayne, shaking his head sadly. "Sometimes I despaired of you, even though I feel sorry to this day, the number of times you was skinned alive. I tell you there was a couple of years, starting about four when I should have thought your mother'd of wore out her arm."

The wickedness of his childhood as remembered by Tom made him sweat. How grateful he should be to his mother for her unstinting purging of the Devil, and he wondered why he wasn't. He wondered also why he felt more shameful pleasure than repentance in these early misdeeds: the time Wayne was caught, on hands and knees, investigating with lustful eyes Mattie, the two-year-old daughter of an itinerant laborer, while the child squatted to relieve herself; the time he was caught in the haymow peering through a crack watching the mating of mare and stallion; the time he'd been knocked almost senseless by his father who came on him trying to peer under the kitchen curtain when his mother was bathing!

These and a flood of other incidents, which Wayne had lost in his unconscious, when revived in detail, were horrifyingly fascinating. Two incidents he remembered on his own, and somehow they became associated in his mind.

One was when he was five. He had been playing in the edge of a pine thicket with Herman Fluger, his own age, and Daisy Hester, a few months his junior, when he was seized with an irresistible impulse to unbutton his pants and exhibit himself.

Herman backed away and turned to explore the horizon, expecting parental wrath to descend in smoking reprisal. He never once turned his eyes back to Wayne and Daisy.

For the little girl it was a fascinating display, and her interest gave Wayne all the pleasure the impulse had anticipated. If Daisy had so much as moved, he'd have instantly covered himself, but her absorbed, round-eyed wonder made him warm and comfortable and extremely pleased with himself. He felt love and tenderness for Daisy.

"I'm going home," Herman had said uncomfortably, and the rebuke in his voice communicated itself. Daisy got to her feet, and, of course, that ended it.

Actually it only began it for Wayne because Herman told his mother who told Daisy's mother, who went to Wayne's mother. Mrs. Morgan, trembling with rage, yanked Wayne out to a scrub cedar behind the cabin and tied him there with a halter rope, saying she could hardly keep her hands off him; that he wasn't fit to run loose and therefore he could stay tethered like a vicious dog until his father came in from work and decided the punishment.

His father was mad. He whipped Wayne with a harness strap and sent him to bed without supper. The next morning Wayne was informed that because Daisy had abetted him by "looking" and not reporting to her mother, he and Daisy no longer were permitted to play together. Herman was a hero.

The other incident was the first time Wayne had an erection to recognize it as something of moment. He ran to his mother feeling somehow it was too much pleasure not to be abnormal, and the expression on her face corroborated his worst fears.

"Put it away," she said in a scandalized voice.

"But what shall I *do*?" he cried panic-stricken.

"I don't know," said the hysterical woman, "put cold water on it!" She yanked up his pants and gave him a sharp wallop on his posterior. "Stop thinking about such things!" She shoved him from the room and slammed the door.

Old Man Starr invariably ended these historical sketches with a compliment: "How you ever turned out to be such a fine young man beats me. I wouldn't have given you two mustard seeds for your soul in them days; but now look at you! The only young man in the Yaate with a real hankering after God!"

What Is Happiness?

Wayne didn't stop by the milking barn until he'd unharnessed his team and thrown down enough hay for night and morning feedings, for his own and the other four teams which would be coming in presently. Then he filled the outdoor mangers high with the loose, dry, fragrant mountain grass and clover and saw to it the watering trough ran full. All the while Old Man Starr's voice came to him as a wonderful soothing evensong from somewhere out of the purple depths of Heaven itself.

When he finally sought out Tom, the old man was on his fifteenth cow, with two to go; and he was quoting scripture.

"Vengeance is mine, saith the Lord," he was admonishing the tail end of Lucy Bell from his seat at her flank. He broke off cheerfully at sight of Wayne. "Evening, Wayne! How's the haying coming?"

"We'll be ready to start hauling day after tomorrow, this weather keeps up."

"We'll call upon the Lord," said the old man.

"What's this about 'vengeance is mine'?" Wayne wanted to know, sitting on one of the ten-gallon cans.

"I was just thinking about that Susie Bates and that P&X Mill worker."

57

Wayne's face darkened.

"I see you already know about it."

Wayne nodded but still said nothing.

"Full as a young jug with a cork in it, I hear, and strutting like she had a corncob a-tween her legs! Shameless! You know that P&X boy?"

"Jack Olsen?"

"Now there's a hoe-handle God could do without!" Tom finished stripping and rose, held out the foaming pail. "Dump this in the strainer whilst I brush down Kitty."

Wayne took the pail and poured the warm milk through the clean porous cloth held with clothespins, while Tom got a stiff brush from the spiderwebbed window sill and brushed Kitty, the last cow, vigorously. She was older than most of the herd, wide from many calves, settled and indifferent.

"You'd think Kitty'd been raised in a hog lot," the old man grumbled. "If there's a pile of manure or a mud waller on the place, that's where she's gonna put it down; flank plastered, bag filthy, and tits caked until they look like a chimblysweep's poker. Some cows like to waller in filth the way some women do. Ungodly!"

After brushing, he took a gunny sack and wiped her udder and teats until they shone pink and clean.

"And they just plain don't care," he glared at Kitty, her eyes closed, chewing her cud benignly. "Dirty today and dirty tomorrow! Much chance of making a self-respecting, Godfearing critter out of her as putting butter up a wild cat with a hot awl."

Wayne laughed! The old man took the emptied pail and

his stool and settled beside Kitty.

"Pity is, she'll fill this three-gallon pail until it brims over, tonight and again tomorrow morning. And that's always perplexed me in cows *and* humans. Dirty cows give more milk and the blasphemers make more money. Howsomever," he philosophized, "money ain't happiness."

"What *is* happiness?" Wayne asked doubtfully.

"Well, I'll tell you what *my* idea of happiness is," answered Tom readily. "To stand on Mt. Baldy some stormy afternoon and see every last one of them Sodomites and Gomorrahites up on the Ridge wiped out with blue bolts of lightning delivered personally by the hand of God Almighty. That'd make me real happy."

Wayne stirred restlessly. "You ever been up on the Ridge?"

"Once," said Tom, "and when I came down I wiped my shoes in quicklime to kill the contamination, and I stood at the pig lot for an hour to get the stench of mortal sin out of my nostrils."

The old man wasn't talking about the Ridge proper. He was referring to the fringe area which consisted of a combination saloon, gambling den, and dance hall, and the "bear pit," a conglomeration of eight or ten dilapidated log huts in a partial clearing, thrown up for the girls and facetiously misnamed the "bare pit."

It was a primitive lure, but on Saturday night, according to Romeo, "the pit was alive as maggots in a dead coyote's testicles."

"A hell-hole for the unwary, the misguided and the misbegotten," was Tom's pronouncement. The clientele was mainly the lumber and mill men, loggers, truckers,

miners, trappers, farm hands, and even elements from Kalispell, Troy, and Bonner's Ferry, eighty to a hundred miles
away. They drank moonshine, danced with what passed on
the Ridge for B-girls and lost their pay checks at the poker
tables and in the pit.

This was only the front door to the real Ridge which
was open to nobody. When the Sheriff wanted anyone from
back yonder, he sent in word.

The original settlers maybe came in with Ezra Meeker
or soon after; long before anyone had opened the Yaate.
Probably two or three malcontent families had broke off
from some wagon train on its way to the Oregon country.
Why they picked such a barren eagle's eyrie with all the
great open West to choose from is not recorded, but here
they put down their unwholesome roots and bred and
interbred until nobody knew who was who, nor how many.

The men were mean, unsavory critters with receding
chins, and the girls were a slovenly, loutish lot; that is, the
first families were like that. The crops off the baby farms was
something different; just as wild, lawless, amoral, and unapproachable, but not physically marked and not so degenerate.

The baby farms came about through a natural sequence
of circumstances. The Ridge had the only midwives at the
time the Yaate was first populated and no doctor available.
When some early Yaates girl got herself in trouble, the
midwife offered to take the unpopular infant. It set a pattern
which Yaaters adhere to even now.

How the Ridge people maintained themselves no one
really knew, except they depended entirely on their own
efforts for survival, as they have done from the beginning.
No one ever saw a Ridger on the Outside except a midwife
on call, or an occasional girl from a baby farm, who hired
herself out to an upcountry trapper or isolated small farmer
to "keep his house" for the winter. That was the formal way

of putting it. And no employer ever registered a complaint, except a Ridge girl was mother-dirty and her cooking was slop. But show me an immaculate Yaate bachelor or one not capable of cooking his own grub. She was more company than a dog and on the bedstead at night just as warm and agreeable as an "armful of princess."

A combination saloon and dance hall was the most recent of the Ridge's enticements. Among those most bitter against it were Max Shoemaker, who furnished a good deal of the moonshine the Yaaters drank, and Old Man Starr, who went up and down the valley calling it the trap door to Hell. He said it so loud and so often *in* meeting and *out*, that pretty soon everybody was referring to the saloon as the Trap Door to Hell. It got to the Ridge, and somebody painted a sign and put it over the door. Now from the Canadian border, west to Spokane, south to Sand Point, Idaho and east to Butte, everybody knew about the Trap Door to Hell.

"Every other boy over eighteen in the Yaate goes to the Ridge," Wayne muttered morosely, helping Tom unlock the stanchions and let the cows out into the night pasture, and then standing by to lug the ten-gallon cans to the root cellar where the cream was separated and cooled and where butter was made and cheese ripened.

"Hell's so full of Yaaters you can see their feet a-sticking out the windows! You hold your convictions, Son, and one day you'll marry yourself a prize girl like your Ma and be a pride to the countryside the way your Pa is."

Tom had been scraping and brooming the droppings and splatterings from the cows into the manure trench and generally tidying up for morning. Seeing Wayne standing by, he said: "I'll take care of the milk tonight! You've had a blessed long day haying. Go along up and eat the vittles the hired girl's got waiting for you."

Wayne paid no heed. "You know any prize girls in the Yaate?" he asked.

Tom put on his coat and stepped between two of the milk cans. "Funny you should mention it," he said, "but have you noticed that towhead young'un of Widder Corvell of late?"

Wayne was bent to lift the second two cans. He straightened and stared.

"Oh, I know she ain't there *yet*, but I was a-noticin' her at meeting this morning, and she ain't got far to go—fifteen ain't she?"

Wayne didn't know; he was barely conscious there was such a person.

"That's what I make her! Fifteen! Come sixteen, and some young feller's going to have hisself the best the Yaate can offer, and what I admire most is the way Widder Corvell rides herd on her. She may be poor as last winter's fodder, but the Widder's got proper pride and prejudice; and she and the girl never miss Sunday Services."

"I wasn't thinking about getting married."

"Them that don't pick won't get no feathers." The old man grasped the inside handles of the two eighty-pound cans of milk and walked off as though they was barely burdensome. Wayne followed with the second two, walking solidly, but not unduly hampered.

Inside the dark cellar Old Man Starr fumbled to light the Coleman lamp, and Wayne set the hand-turned separator to spinning.

"Sixteen!" Wayne protested as Tom poured out the contents of the first can.

"It's not only allowable but preferable," Tom admonished. "Yaate cherries got to be picked early before the pests get at 'em!"

Strike Him Dead

That night after he had gone to bed Wayne tried to remember the face of the Widow Corvell's daughter. He couldn't, but out of deep nowhere her name suddenly came floating up to him. Eve! He felt buoyed up, elated and all at once content. He slept sweetly without nightmares.

When Sunday came again, the haying was out of the way and although the Rev. Mr. Grocer wasn't due, Wayne went to Service with Mr. and Mrs. Morgan and young Hal, and sat well down front with the ranking Christians. He saw Old Man Starr's white head at the back of the congregation where a hired hand would naturally sit, and somewhere between he found Eve Corvell and her mother. He dare not stare over his shoulder, and was pleasantly astonished.

Without the Rev. Mr. Grocer, the informal service was Bible study, hymns and prayer, ending with a half-hour of personal testimonials. Tom Starr was in his glory, interjecting "hallelujahs" and "amens" until the rafters rang; and in his turn stood up and boomed out his story of salvation and the consolation thereof.

After the meeting there was a general lingering in the churchyard as though these isolated neighbors hungered for just a few minutes more communion. Wayne got his first full look at Eve and was suffused with a pleasant warmth. Tom had called her a towhead young'un but her hair was golden in the sunshine, and she was not at all the child Wayne had supposed. He had encountered Eve almost every

Sunday and on Friday mail day since the Corvells had come to Yaates Valley five years before, but only saw her now.

She stood with a group of girls her own age, and to Wayne's mind she was as superior as Tom had said.

When the Morgans had taken their places at the opening of Services, Wayne had been surprised to see Jack Olsen from the P&X Mill seated with Susie Bates and her father and mother. He thought it queer unless Susie had won her point and Jack had given in to marrying her.

Now outside, Wayne saw Susie cross to the group of girls, and he looked about for Olsen. The burly, over-muscled young man, looking tight and uncomfortable in his flashy store suit, was leaning against a tree watching the girls with an expression unseemly in a man who had cut his favorite from the herd and already put his brand on her.

Suddenly Wayne realized it wasn't the group Jack was appreciating, but Eve. A passion of jealous rage grabbed him by the throat and shook him till his teeth chattered. He was grateful Old Man Starr joined him at that moment. Tom hadn't noticed. He nodded toward Jack Olsen and said with satisfaction, "Now that them two's made their crop, looks like they aim to build a fence about it."

"Let's go home," said Wayne thickly.

Old Man Starr looked surprised.

"Ain't you gonna ride with your folks, the way you come?"

"I'd rather walk with you."

"And welcome."

Wayne was silent until they'd cleared the forest trees

and were on the open upland. Finally he said, "That Olsen hasn't got his mind on Susie Bates."

"He better have," Tom replied grimly. "He was at meeting with the Bates family this morning for no other reason than Fred Bates threatened to blow his head off, if he didn't mean business."

"I didn't know that." Wayne felt a surge of relief.

"Fred laid down the law he was to attend Services with the family for the next two Sundays and then show up when Preacher Grocer comes next, with a marriage license."

"That's more than Fred Bates has ever done before."

"Well, he said he was sick and tired of having every dog's meat for a daughter, but I think the real reason is that Susie's fixed her mind on Jack Olsen, and she's hounded Fred into it."

"Well, Jack's mind's not on it."

"You know for a fact?"

"He had his eyes glued to Eve Corvell this morning," Wayne said savagely.

"May God strike him dead." There was shock in the old man's voice.

"And Tom," there was a note of rising hysteria despite Wayne's effort for control, "if he touches that girl I'm going to kill him."

"And I'll hold him while you do it." The old man looked and sounded like Moses on Sinai with the thunder of God rolling about him and the lightning of God's wrath striking about his white bearded head.

Wayne had never seen Tom so disturbed. The old man's stern acquiescence to his threat frightened him. He actually hadn't thought of *doing* murder when he spoke his emotion, but somehow Tom's approval put God's seal on it. In truth, Old Man Starr wasn't thinking of murder either. He was expressing moral indignation. Personally, when he wanted a job of dirty work done, he had always called upon the Almighty to handle it for him.

Bears is Skittish

The following week Tom and Wayne were several miles up on Huckleberry Ridge getting the family's share of the purple drops of fruit before the bears cleaned them out, when Romeo McFeddor popped through the brush, his thirty-ought-eight lollying across his arm.

"Bears is skittish this year," he commented after an opening greeting, "and deer is worse."

"You mistake a yearling heifer, and Mr. Bates'll run your tail plumb out of the country," Old Man Starr warned.

Romeo gathered a handful of berries and crammed them in his grinning maw. He wasn't above poaching now and again when meat was scarce.

"Interesting situation down below," he said by way of changing a delicate subject. "That P&X Mill boy who blew up Susie Bates was at the Gambles' barn raising last night. How come you wasn't there?" This last was to Wayne. A shadow crossed Wayne's face, but he merely said:

"I was packing grub into the sheep camp yesterday. Didn't get back in time."

"Well, sir, you missed something! That there Olsen boy was paying court to the Widder Corvell something lively; bringing her lemonade, handing her the plate supper and generally making a nuisance of hisself. Course, everybody knowed you got to salt the cow to catch the calf."

Wayne grabbed up his pail of berries and walked off through the brush.

"What's bit him?" Romeo was amazed.

Tom, as upset as Wayne, blazed out: "If you ever get to be a bigger liar you'll have to take on weight!"

Romeo set back on his heels, scratched his chin reflectively.

"Honest to my Grandma, Starr," he said, "there's days when you're barely fit to be tied up. That's what a man gets for living alone with God, doubtless."

The old man turned his back and went on picking berries, but his hand shook.

"All I was gonna say," Romeo went on in an injured tone, "was that Susie Bates seen the lay of the land and flung a whingding that edified the occasion considerable. Went after her pappy's deer gun in the car. Jack Olsen sure hit for home faster'n he come."

Still Tom went on picking, giving no evidence of having heard. Romeo stood uncertain:

"Well, for Christ's sake, is that all you got to say?" He strode off in disgust.

On his way home Old Man Starr came on Wayne lying under a tree, face down, so quiet at first he thought the boy was asleep. He wasn't. He arose heavily, and the two walked silently for a long piece.

"Romeo McFeddor's a born liar," Tom said at last.

Wayne just looked at him and the old man shut up.

That night Wayne was convulsed by such a nightmare that it awakened his whole family, and was not himself until his father threw a pitcher of water over him and hauled him out of his bunk.

The next afternoon Jack Olsen dragged in from the slashing where he'd been burning brush, bruised, battered, and trampled until his ma wouldn't have him. Several of the millhands got him to the bunkhouse and out of his tatters and into his sougans. All he would say was that he'd tangled with a she-bear with cubs. There were no signs of claw or teeth marks, and the millhands were puzzled. It was two days before he was up and about. During his brooding convalescence a vengeful spirit was actively at work.

The Saturday night he was back on his feet, he went to the Ridge with four or five of his intimates. Casually he brought the conversation around to Wayne Morgan. As always there was a spate of ribald comment.

"Give you even money, if you was to strip off his pants you'd find his pocket empty of seeds."

"Well, you love God, you can't love women."

"Wouldn't he raise hell in the Bear Pit!"

This was what Jack Olsen had been waiting for. "Why don't we try it and see?"

The plotters fell to exploring the idea with a lively mixture of deviltry and mountain whiskey. Olsen let the others plan and explore the idea, but guided them until the whole diabolical skein was woven to his satisfaction. Wayne would be lured out, kidnapped and brought to the Ridge, and locked in one of the Bear Pit cabins with a naked whore. The plotters anticipated the rest could be left to the girl and nature. Olsen knew just the girl for the job. She would be intrigued. Afterwards the Yaates would resound with mocking laughter. It appealed as a hell of an idea.

Now, although Wayne had sought him out and picked a quarrel, Olsen had not the faintest suspicion of the truth behind his antagonist's truculence. He supposed Wayne had overheard some slighting remarks pertaining to his prissy masculinity. God knows, there had been enough of them; the Morgan boy and his abstinence was a standard butt for sly insinuations.

Wayne had acted on a driving impulse, had hunted Olsen down, challenged him, beat him with uncontrollable fury, and then went home relieved, but with misgiving. He hadn't come out of the fracas entirely unscathed and when Old Man Starr heard that Jack Olsen had been mauled by a bear, he looked at Wayne with added interest, but kept silent.

In His Madness

Work hours what they were and distance in the Yaates what it was, it wasn't until the following Friday mail day that Olsen was able to have a word with Wayne, which was in effect that the latter had fouled him on the previous encounter and he challenged him to try again the next evening, Saturday night.

Wayne was at the point of ignoring him when Olsen lost interest and went to meet Mrs. Corvell and Eve as they arrived at the steps of the Federal Building. That settled it. He drew Olsen aside and tersely fixed the time and place, savagely agreeing, that as before, no one else should be drawn into the affair.

Wayne's morose restlessness all day Saturday communicated itself to Tom Starr as forewarning of impending trouble. Dusk was a thin silky veil, but still would not be blue velvet for yet another hour when Wayne brought out his cow-pony and set off. The old man had just finished the milking. Having a good notion that Wayne had Jack Olsen on his mind, he set out across country on a barely passable deer trail, which foreshortened the conventional route to the P&X Mill by several miles.

He called on God aloud and fervently, breathlessly quoting scripture as he toiled and sweated over the rugged terrain, much too perturbed for hymn singing. He hurried faster than an old man should travel in the hills, but he arrived at the clearing behind the mill only to see the pony cantering off homeward without a rider and Wayne with a potato sack over his head, feet and hands bound, being loaded into a jeep by six masked men, and whisked off up the Ridge cut-off.

He yelled and shook his fist and called down God's wrath in his impotence; then with the return of common sense, cut across a ravine and over the brow of a hill, hoping still to circle the runaway pony. He found the animal browsing about a mile down the road and after a little maneuvering, caught up the dragging reins. Mounting, he turned the horse after the long-departed jeep and whipped the astonished animal into a lather. With his white hair standing on end in the wind and his saintly beard flying in the dying light, he had the blurred semblance of the Avenging Angel on horseback, and no time to spare.

The leading entourage arriving at the edge of the Ridge clearing, parked in the shadows away from the lights of the Trap Door to Hell. Amid stealthy whispers and excited chuckles, two of the six went ahead to guard against witnesses and the other four carried their squirming, muffled burden to one of the more distant cabins in the Bear Pit.

There were two girls waiting instead of the prearranged one. They greeted the arrivals with laughter, and the hilarity increased when the pranksters stripped Wayne to his drawers, the potato sack still over his head. Then retying his hands and feet, they dumped the ludicrous figure on the bed, at the mercy of the two women, and withdrew, locking the door behind them.

Before removing the sack the women were not above a little preliminary fun of their own, but when Wayne of a sudden stiffened strangely and then collapsed and lay as though dead, they became frightened and jerked off the bag.

The boy had lost consciousness perhaps from lack of air, or maybe from fear and excessive emotion. The older of the two girls had the sense to cut the bonds of his hands and feet and sent the other to bring a basin of water.

In a moment Wayne opened his eyes, wild and staring. It took him a full fifty seconds to regain his faculties and realize he was lying between two anxious females, mother-naked, and himself little better off.

With an insane bellow he leaped from the bed and lunged at the door. It was solid. Now that he was a man again, the girls watched with amusement from the bed and inveigled him in endearing terms. In his madness Wayne turned on them, grabbed the great oldfashioned oak bed by the sideboards, upsetting bedclothes, mattress, springs and terrified girls in a hodgepodge scramble on the floor. With superhuman strength he tore a heavy leg from the headboard and with this weapon, broke the lock on the door.

Tom Starr met him half a mile from the Ridge, fleeing down the road in socks and drawers, pursued by no one but the Devil himself. Wayne passed him without pause or recognition, and it took Tom another half mile to catch him and make himself known to the witless boy.

Had anyone been on the backroads and byways leading up to Grizzly Flat and the Morgan ranch that night, he would have witnessed in the moonlight the strangest apparition of all his numbered days: an hysterical young man in a fit of ague, clad only in his drawers, riding double in the arms of a praying patriarch right out of the Old Testament.

Thick as Thieves

Whether it was from fear of repercussion for that Saturday prank; or Susie Bates' father's rifle; or just that the P&X Mill was coming to the slow season, Jack Olsen packed his ditty-bag and departed from Yaates Valley that same weekend.

Inasmuch as the plan had misfired, the other plotters were glad to pretend it had never happened; and being the two girls were not paid to talk, Wayne's trip to the Ridge never came to general gossip. But Old Man Starr brooded over the affair, and his resentment against the Trap Door to Hell in particular and the Ridge in general grew apace.

While Tom mourned over the unpredictable ways of the Devil, Wayne brooded over Eve Corvell. The blurred provocative incitement of the Bear Pit had inflamed him beyond human tolerance.

Wayne worked his father's fields like a man with two hoes. There were days when he wandered the rugged back country, waded icy streams, burst through buck brush, challenged peaks and sheer cliffs, driven by devils who rode him unceasingly until he dropped exhausted, scratched, bruised and drenched by creek water and his own perspiration; sobbing with bursting lungs.

All the while his mind shied away from the two naked whores on the bed and fixed with increasing greediness on the face of Eve. He had no notion where he traveled on these self-punishing outings, what direction he took nor why.

Once he threw himself down in blind exhaustion beneath the Gallows Tree. It was a small rocky clearing not far off the Salt Creek road and was a gaunt lightning-struck ironwood tree, dead since memory of man. The Gallows Tree in a sense substitutes for the conventional haunted houses of other areas, and is the center of a horde of apocryphal stories. One of the stories says three Indians were hung from its limbs for horse thievery; another that a young girl hanged herself here after her illegitimate child had been taken from her and sent up on the Ridge; another that enraged pioneers had hanged a man and his daughter here for living in open and flagrant sin.

Wayne brooded long under the tree and that night his nightmares rode him unconscionably. Next Sunday when the Rev. Mr. Grocer invited those whose souls were especially heavy down front to the mourners' bench, he came and cried out for succor.

In a roundabout way, it was Romeo McFeddor who opened Eve Corvell's eyes to Wayne's interest. He had put two polecats together up at the huckleberry patch, and hatched a real little stinker of an idea. When he came down that afternoon he stopped by Seth Bascomb's place.

"Hal Morgan's oldest boy finally got his 'he' glands out of tissue paper," he remarked.

"Wayne?" Seth was surprised.

"He's set to spread his tailfeathers for Widder Corvell's gal."

"He say so?"

"He might as well of! You see the look on his face last

Friday mail day?"

Seth hadn't, but he was watching at Sunday Services, and he agreed. He mentioned it to the Rev. Mr. Grocer, and the good reverend made a fatuous remark to Mrs. Corvell. Eve's mother was flabbergasted, but most agreeably pleased. In no time the word was around.

Eve was titillated and in the following weeks watched Wayne with shy approachable smiles. It soon became an accepted fact that there was an understanding without Wayne ever having to do any spadework.

Of course, Eve wouldn't be sixteen until the following June, but who wouldn't agree she was worth waiting for, and they'd make a handsome couple. Now, the gossip ran, it was understandable why Wayne had kept himself aloof. He was going to follow in his father's footsteps and be a substantial family man and a credit to the countryside. He was a fine, intelligent, hard-working, admirable young man; and the Yaate was proud of him.

Old Man Starr knew better. That terrible night on the Ridge had done something to Wayne and hatred burned in Tom's heart. Or perhaps it was jealousy! Before, Wayne had been a confidant; in a manner of speaking, a son. Now Wayne was black, difficult and withdrawn.

The week after the news spread of Wayne's interest in Eve, Tom spent an entire Saturday night on his knees wrestling with the Lord, and the next day he was not at Sunday Services. This was an event, but was forgotten when word came down from the Ridge that the Trap Door to Hell had blown up, and along with it the bartender-owner, the bouncer, two prostitutes and Lukey Pierce, a Spider Creek rancher.

This was important enough to bring in the Sheriff from the county seat. He sniffed around but couldn't make head nor tail of it and got precious little help either from Yaaters or Ridgers. He finally gave it as his opinion that the oversized still under the saloon had blown up, and went home.

Nobody felt one way or the other about the owner, the bouncer or the two girls, and the consensus of opinion was that Lukey Pierce should have been at home with Mrs. Pierce and his three kids. They gave a suitable funeral for Lukey out of sympathy for Mrs. Pierce, but the Sheriff's men had to collect what they could rake up of the two men and one of the girls and take them down to the county seat for burial at the county's expense. The other girl had vanished entirely, apparently whisked off by the Devil, clothes and all.

Seth Bascomb was disgusted with the Sheriff. He told Romeo, "Them folks down at the county seat don't know a boiler explosion from a stick of dynamite, and that shows pretty plain what politics is."

Romeo just grinned. "Better that way," he said philosophically.

"But you can still smell blasting powder up yonder," Seth protested, "and all you got to do is look at the way the building caved in to know that somebody put about ten sticks of high-grade powder in the fireplace. Exploded still!" There was a snort of supreme scorn in Seth's old nostrils.

"Well," Romeo pointed out, "you could have spoke up and said your piece. You had the chanst."

Seth just looked at Romeo and clamped his jaws shut.

"How you reckon it was done?"

Seth shrugged, "Ain't the first time augur holes been bored into the end of a fireplace log and filled up with dynamite and fuse caps."

Romeo concurred.

"Happened early in the evening. The primed log was probably already on the irons when a match was touched to the evening fire. Got any ideas?"

Seth shook his head.

But Romeo had ideas the next day when Max Shoemaker came down from Salt Creek with the soaking wet body of Old Man Starr on the tail of his logging truck. They lifted him off and laid him on the porch of Seth's cabin. He looked as benign and patriarchal in death as in life.

"I was fishing in the big pool up by the Turn-Off, and there he was bobbing face down in an eddy. Not a mark on him," Max said.

"Suicide?" asked Romeo.

Max shrugged. Seth rose from his kneeling position and looked at Romeo argumentatively.

"Why you want to say a thing like that?"

"Well, Old Man Starr and God was thick as thieves. I just thought maybe him and God did one last job together and then the old man up and joined his sidekick."

Seth looked down at the still figure for a thoughtful moment and then went inside to the Forest Service phone to notify the Coroner at the county seat, so they could get the old man buried before he started to bloat up, the way drowned bodies sometimes do.

PART IV

The Resurrection

First realization of horror came to Marty in the flickering darkness of the forest cabin with the slow, painful sound of laborious panting outside, and the shuffling, inch by inch, of some cumbersome object across the porch, a heavy, wearisome effort as might be made by a wounded creature dragging its paralyzed hindquarters.

Marty's gaunt young body quivered under the reflex shock of disbelief as a guilty conscience might feel dismay on sudden exposure. A fine cold spray of sweat suffused the girl, dampening her rough cotton nightgown; making her flesh crawl under the unkempt pile of worn sougans on the bunk bed.

Perception was animal-keen to have heard those fumbling, futile sounds above the insistent driving deluge of the March Montana rain; and especially above the bass viol baying of the high mountain equinoctial wind through the Lodgepole pines with the constant obligato of higher shrieks and yapping of the storm two hundred feet above, in the tops of the Tamarack and Larch.

Without warning the decayed, neglected tooth at the back of Marty's jaw began to throb dully, and a swollen wrist joint, from a week-old accident, began to ache. Second by second, her bunk bed of mental anguish was becoming, as well, a nightmarish bed of physical torment.

Tension was stiffening her joints in acute arthritic agony; vivid streaks of neuralgic head pains flashed with lightning-like irregularity and intensity through her skull; her breathing was almost as labored as the gasping outside the door.

Such moral and physical dissolution Marty had not known, even in "The Worst Days," not in all her nineteen years. This was her fifth in the most primitive area of Yaates Valley, seventy miles by dirt road to the nearest town; three to four miles by footpath through Lodgepole thickets to the nearest neighbor.

Five years toward a life sentence of self-imposed isolation had furtively tiptoed past, undemanding, unheeded, since Max had dragged her from under that Spokane bridge, a furious little wildcat of fourteen; had bundled her in a roll of sougans in the cab of his logging truck; strapped her down; put a dirty red bandana between her teeth and got her across two state lines while eyewitnesses were still calling the authorities.

For a whole year she saw no other but Max; except once a government timber cruiser way off across the big mountain meadow on the Forest Service road. Up and down the Yaates Valley it was understood that Max had gone into Spokane and got himself a woman.

On her fifteenth birthday she looked old enough, so Max took her in to the county seat, passed her off for eighteen, and married her as a birthday present. That was the way Max was! No particular reason. He just did it; just as on a whim he'd snatched her from the brink in Spokane.

Max hazed a logging truck up and down the Montana

mountain roads for a living. He was sometimes away so long Marty wondered whether he would come back. All she ever knew was he delivered logs to Bonners' Ferry, to Kalispell, to Sand Point, Idaho, and once in a while over to Spokane. Ten days, two weeks, even a month was no time at all for Max to be on the road.

And then when the logging was slack, there were long absences back somewhere in the real Primitive Area at the liquor still; or for unaccountable periods, poaching out-of-season grouse and venison for favored Outlanders. So, in season and out, Marty was mostly alone, and one way or another, it didn't matter.

In these years of isolation, it had never entered Marty's conscious mind to expect anything other than she found; loneliness, fear, or unhappiness were beyond the horizon of her world. Her shell by now was impregnable against the physical world, and all but the shallowest sensations. She neither felt the winter sub-zero cold, nor the raw wet chill of fall, nor spring rains and hailstones, nor summer heat. Hunger, pain, friendlessness, shabbiness, were lost on her; and so, too, were their opposites: the ecstacy of healthy appetites; the sensuous luxury of warmth; the authentic beauty of cleanliness; the cheerfulness of human associations.

She neither knew nor cared or differentiated between the good and the wicked; between gratitude and meanness; between satiety and emptiness. It was so with Max's love-making. It was there or it wasn't, and she made no effort to remember which. She ate without choice or distinction; taking from the cupboard what canned or boxed stuff Max put there from time to time. The door of each passing moment closed behind Marty the instant she had passed through. No yesterday, no tomorrow. She breathed, she ate, she drank, she moved; but then so did the Lodgepole pine.

She looked out on the world with soulless eyes of indifference; her countenance a stony mask. Even alone in this remoteness, she was not given to private conscious thought. Her guarding ego did not allow it. Marty was adrift in a vacuum, vague, unaware, unresponsive. Perhaps, sitting under a hot August sun on the bank of the Yaates River, there might come a momentary softening around her lips, a lassitude in her limbs, or even an instant of dreaminess in her eyes. But these were flickering, unguarded moments, vanishing as Marty awakened to remember that she was Marty.

Her indifference extended endlessly; through the stream of meaningless daylight hours and through the ceaseless flow of unmarked nights; through storms, through floods, washed-out roads, even through the nightly prowl of predatory wild life, sniffing and grunting about the chinked logs; clawing at the door; investigating the windows—heavily barred against just such mischief or mischance.

One winter night a veritable prehistoric monster of a grizzly had stood on his hind legs and raked the double-thick Tamarack shakes from the cabin roof, nine feet above the ground, and withdrew to tear up a half-acre of Lodgepole pines before he died of Marty's two 30.06 dumdum slugs directly between the eyes. Even that night had been met with stoicism, and slid out of Marty's memory with the rest.

Then what was so frightening tonight, in the small futile sounds coming out of the night's fury?

Some reflex compelled Marty out of her bunk and to the door. She knew the bar was in place but she fumbled to make sure, as she made sure of the key in the metal lock. Now she grasped the knob as though by her handgrip alone, she could prevent invasion.

The labored breathing on the storm-lashed porch was heartbreaking and fearsome, but the dragging had ceased. Of a sudden Marty's scalp tingled, icy sweat trickled down her spine; her bare feet could not have been colder had she stood knee-deep in a snow bank!

Something, hand, paw or claw—whether thing, human or subhuman—that haunted the door, had grasped the knob and the pressure was so animal-strong that, despite Marty's grip of terror, it turned in her hand. But, the door locked and barred, made the turning futile. Still, for Marty, the knob was a potent conductor, sending petrifying shocks of terror flowing over the metal path through the door. The girl was transfixed; she could release herself no more than a lineman caught on a high tension wire. Then, from without, there was a hoarse, mournful sigh—a hopeless resignation—and the knob was released. In that moment Marty was set free. She flamed, out of horror and terror, into the ball of fury Max had captured under the Spokane bridge, all teeth, nails, and madness.

Max's 30.06 was on the deer antlers over the fireplace where she'd replaced it at two-thirty this afternoon. Actually, all day had been a bleak, damp-aired dusk in anticipation of the storm now raging. Risking the halfhearted flickers on the hearth that might still silhouette her, Marty grasped the rifle and fled back to the shadow of her bunk. Instinctively she opened the gun, and checked the chamber, as Max had taught her, and snapped off the safety.

For what seemed an eternity, the breathing on the porch was suspended. It began again, more desperately animal than ever, and with it, a retreating shuffle and drag across the rough porch floor.

Marty kept her ears attuned to the movement on the porch, but her eyes went instinctively to the multipaned window across the cabin, still faintly showing in the firelight. By now the withdrawal had reached the railing; now the three steps. And then all sound ceased as the inarticulate creature pulled itself off into the night's turbulence.

Now the question becomes more insistent! How do we

reconcile this passionately terrorized girl with the Marty so long impervious to emotional stimulus; so insensitive and insensible to all physical, mental or moral forces? This haunting devastation; this uncontrollable fear-ridden moment could have risen only out of the girl herself! It had to be something basic and fundamental to Marty's very essence to shatter a five-year wall of subhuman indifference.

Marty screamed, half rising to fire blindly at the window, and then, with an epileptic twisting and jerking, she slipped to the floor, unconscious.

The 30.06 bored a neat, unsplintered hole through one of the small top panes, missing widely the gaunt suffering face pressed against a lower frame. It was a classic death's-head, even to the shreds of leaves in the hair, and the graveyard silt on its brow and cheeks. If ever a man had risen from his own grave, this unwholesome creature had. And in truth, until one hour ago, Oscar Fergusen *had* been secure in his unmarked grave, buried and unmourned.

Such a Safe World

When Marty was thirteen she was a normal, sheltered child of a respectable upper middle-class Spokane family, wholly unprepared for and defenseless against her first and almost fatal dose of worldly knowledge. The bitter capsule was forced between her teeth with the realization that her mother and father actually were not "One"; that family entity was not universal and indestructible.

This was Marty's first terror; the sudden knowledge that a father often was more concerned with his own frustrations than with the needs of his family. And because fathers were so made, there was no stability nor security in home life.

Marty's second terror was catastrophic. Forced to face the flimsy frailty of this shaky family structure, there was panic in her soul; but six months after, when she and her mother and sister had endured all the bitter, ugly barrenness of desertion, came the agonizing discovery that mothers without the steadying hand of a husband were nothing but an ill-natured, undirected feminine hunger, without emotional stability or moral stamina. That is when Marty's whole world dissolved into a gray, murky void.

What did all the joyful childhood, which had gone before, amount to now? What had been its meaning and purpose?

All those bedside prayers; all those breathtaking fairy

tales of truth and honor and goodness her father had read to her; all the kissing and petting and loving her mother and father had done together that had so warmed and delighted her; all the moments of happiness on her mother's knee with her head on her mother's young, ample breast, all the gay songs that she remembered coming from her mother's sweet voice; all the infinite pains her mother's nimble fingers had taken with her own and her sister's starched and embroidered lacy wardrobe, so that they might be equal to any other little girl; all the little lessons in manners, behavior, in modesty, honor and sincerity; all the stress on personal pride and appearance; all the emphasis on the graciousness of living.

Everything had been important to Marty, because each little nicety had had meaning and importance to her mother, father, and the family unity!

Now, when she was thirteen, it was all suddenly nothing. And most of all was the moral weakness of her mother, so stark and shockingly present once her father was gone, that killed Marty's soul.

Within a child's ken it had been such safe, wholesome, comfortable, gracious family living. No real wealth, except the wealth of everything good that belongs to the average-income family in a fairly large northwestern city's pleasant, uncomplicated social activities.

Every weekend her father mowed his lawn with the other family men on their street. On Saturday, her mother did the week's baking of bread, pies, cakes, doughnuts and, sometimes, batches of fudge, pinoche and taffy. In the summer and fall she canned fruits and vegetables, put down pickles in dill and brine, fried up fifty pounds of pork sausage and put the juicy patties down in five-gallon cans of lard. Then there were the jars of shelled almonds and walnuts; and in October, fruitcake and English plum puddings, full of suet, fruit and nuts, generously drenched with brandy, which were put down in the special crocks to mature and ripen for the holidays.

Marty's father worked hard, six days a week, and came home every evening full of exciting "downtown" adventures. He was the merriest of men in Marty's adoring eyes. He laughed and swung Marty's mother until her feet left the ground; loved a good pillow fight with Marty and her sister; sang in the bathroom at the top of his voice; sat at the rusty upright piano and played "Three O'Clock in the Morning" and "Dark Town Strutter's Ball" with gusto and then sat down to dinner with every evidence of pleasure and satisfaction.

The family ritual at the table was of great importance to him, and took on significant form and gravity for Marty and her sister. Even Marty's mother, who loved lightness and laughter, seemed graver, more thoughtful, and yet happiest at this hour of the day.

Marty loved the dinner hour. In fact, she loved all the hours her father and mother were home together. And even when they were going out for the evening, leaving Marty and her sister tucked in bed alone; even then, it wasn't too awful, because her mother and father were together.

She never consciously thought about this, of course, but that's what soothed her and made sleep sweet and possible. The oneness of her mother and father; the completeness of the family circle.

So how was Marty to be prepared for the ugly week when her mother did not come out of her bedroom, or so far as Marty knew, even come out of her bed; but only lay there moaning and crying. And her father simply wasn't there any more. He had come home one evening, and there had been loud, ugly words behind the closed door of the bedroom. Dinner had been a nightmarish ghost of a meal. Her mother's hand trembled as she served; her face red and her eyes bewildered. Her father's face was white and adamant, his manner withdrawn; he was a stranger in the house. There was a strained, staring, unbelieving look on her sister's face, and in her own stomach sat an ugly acid lump, and an icy wind blew over her.

In the morning her father was not there, and her mother did not come out of her bed. It got on towards school time, and there was no breakfast and no lunches put up. Marty and her sister walked from room to room, vague, uncertain, and a little disjoined, like solemn half-grown storks suddenly and self-consciously on elongated legs. Nobody seemed to know they existed, nor cared. There was such a starkness in the house; such deep, forbidding shadows where shadows existed; blinding daylight where the sun came in; everything was harshness, blatant; dead black or garish white.

Marty's sister had a tiny cupboard hideaway in the attic, just large enough for her and her favorite book of the moment. That day, her sister took *Little Women* into the attic cubicle and ran away from what she couldn't face. It would have been so much better for Marty if she, too, had had someplace, someone, or something in which to hide. But Marty wasn't a reader, and she didn't have the instinct of her sister to crawl back into the darkness and safety of the womb. So she just stood out in the open, confused by her terror, her mind numb with what she didn't understand, and sick with disbelief for what she did understand; dying a little with each added moment of suspense, craven with fear for what would happen next.

Divorce In This House

The second day came and went, another aeon of blankness, another horizonless waste of aching void, and then another, and another. At the end of the fifth day, a man came to the door to ask why Marty and her sister were not in school, and Marty heard her sister tell the man, "There is a divorce going on in this house." It sounded to Marty exactly as though her sister had said, "There is a death going on in this house." It must have sounded something of the same to the man, too, because he said, "Oh," in a rather hushed, embarrassed voice, and after an uncertain hesitancy, backed away from the door.

On the morning of the sixth day Marty's mother came out of the bedroom; but it wasn't really her mother, she didn't look like anybody's mother. Her bright, friendly, laughing eyes were heavy, sullen and dull; her complexion, always rosy, was drawn and chalkish white; her long raven hair, her pride and Marty's joy, was loose and frowzy; and instead of the crisp housedresses Marty loved, her mother pushed around in a pair of house slippers, a pink fuzzy nightgown, and an old kimono.

She prepared a breakfast of sorts and slopped it on the table. She didn't pretend to sit down. Neither Marty nor her sister could swallow a bite of it. Not once then, nor ever, did her mother ask how she and her sister had existed those five previous black days. Marty couldn't have said, if she had been asked. She had no sense of having eaten anything, although she did remember being hungry sometimes, and

91

searching the cupboards. Whether she ate what she found, she didn't recall.

On the following Monday, her mother went through the routine motions of getting Marty and her sister ready for school and "fixing" a lunch. But both girls ended up in disorder; their hair dressed with vagueness and fumbling; their clothes higgledy-piddledy, put on them with such lack of pride or concern; their lunch pails held such a show of indifference, that neither girl could face school. Not for an instant did they think of questioning their mother's slothful unconcern.

They left the house as usual, but turned away from the schoolyard and went down to the skid row end of town along the riverfront where no one they knew would see them; and to be even more inconspicuous, they sat under the railroad bridge, out of people's way.

They had their schoolbooks with them, and on the first day there was that heart-rending little compulsion, driving them to do the right thing—to conform—which made them study and hear the other's lessons. They did it earnestly and conscientiously, as though it were of grave importance. Every day that week they went back to the bridge, but each day the compulsion to study, the feeling of the importance of their gesture died a little, and by Friday they simply stuck their books under the front step on their way out of the house and went down to the river unhampered.

It was also on Friday, there under the bridge, that the two girls first sensed the danger of their new freedom. For a week now, they'd been out from under any mature influence; home and family were no more; society hadn't found them yet, and so, for the moment, all legal or lawful solicitude was in abeyance.

For Marty and her sister, their one big ache and their full concern lay in this shocking realization: that they no longer belonged; that they were outside; no continuity, no meaning in anything. They were lost, unimportant bits of castoff flotsam in an unstable sea of social turbulence.

As the girls sat quietly, unobserved in the cool bridge shadows, there came a new knowledge and awareness of a different kind of violence and horror. A young warehouse worker and a blowzy girl slid down under the bridge across the river, maybe fifty feet away, and after several drinks from a pint bottle, indulged in a vivid, completely animal act of copulation.

Marty's sister vomited, but all Marty did was shake as though taken with a chill. Both girls dragged home that afternoon in high fever. They tossed all night, and the next morning even their mother, so wholly engrossed with self-pity and self-commiseration, came out of her fog enough to call a doctor. Both girls were in bed for the better part of a week. Marty recovered first, but remained draggy, indifferent, vapid. Her sister lay in a coma for two days more, at last coming to her senses, she gagged, then vomited. This continued the first thing upon awakening each morning for the next four days. After that, she seemed to get better; but now she read her books as she'd never read before. She crawled off to her hideaway in the attic at every available moment.

Not Marty. When she was well enough, she was drawn back to watch the bridge with a compulsion that was stronger than fear of any known punishment or concern for personal danger. Both girls were back in school, but it was only a gesture. Their mother didn't pretend to care, and the school authorities had enough to keep them busy with the children of parents who did care.

It was in the fourth or fifth month after the divorce that Marty's mother began not to be home. Sometimes she wasn't there after school; sometimes she wasn't there in the evenings. And it was about this time that a boarder was taken into the house. A loud, good-natured, beer-drinking, careless, no-account of a man who was given the run of the house but was supposed to sleep in the guest bedroom. It didn't take Marty long to know that he didn't always sleep where he was supposed to. Her sister saw nothing; knew nothing; walking in the fantasy world of her books. But Marty saw and knew; and lost the last tattered shreds of her soul. Suddenly, she wanted to be filthier than her mother. Nothing would satisfy but that she should fall lower than anyone else. The new boarder sensed it, even before Marty encouraged him. And that's how Marty slid down under the railroad bridge with her first man.

It was through the boarder that Max came into her life. He'd just driven into Spokane from Montana with a double truck of spruce logs. She'd agreed to go with Max down under the railroad bridge....But as they were approaching along the river bank Marty, without warning or premeditation, changed from a docile, indifferent creature into a thing of fury. Before Max was aware of her intent, she had grabbed up a five-pound fieldstone; threw herself upon a woman just coming from under the bridge, beating her with the stone until she crumpled, and then spurned her with a kick so that the woman rolled into the river. That's when Max dragged Marty away, bundled her up in his bedroll of sougans, tied and gagged her, and left Spokane within the hour. He never did know that the woman in the river was Marty's mother.

Lightning Blue-Blazed

It may have been one hour or three after the grotesque face had shown itself in the cabin window that Marty stirred, sat up on the drafty rough-hewn cabin floor, and brought her dazed senses to focus. Her first conscious perception was physical; a sense of bone-chilling cold, and then, immediately, her ears caught the maelstrom outside. The wind was rampant and erratic, twisting, turning, and rushing at the cabin from first one direction and then another; giving a sense of great force and motion, as though the mountain cabin was a ship in a heavy sea. Thunder came first in a voluminous roll, then in a shattering, ear-splitting clatter, seemingly from all sides; snapping and cracking as the lashes of a hundred bullwhips.

Trees moaned and swayed, limbs and treetops snapped and fell like splinter-wood. Now and again, there was an earthshaking shudder, a booming crash, as another forest giant was yanked up by the roots, carrying down scores of smaller trees in its death plunge.

Lightning blue-blazed and sizzled through the forest in its own ghostly light with the malicious teeth of a spitting, frolicking mountain cat. The rain, still falling in sheets, was scooped up by the wind and flung against the cabin with the force of ocean waves.

Marty had never learned to drink the powerful amber stuff Max distilled back in the woods, but the crawly goose-pimple chill on her flesh, the deep cold in her bones, and now the persistent sharper ache of her dying tooth, drove her to it. There was some cold black coffee on the wood stove; she poured a tin cup two-thirds full, put in some sugar, and then, from a gallon jug Max kept behind the woodbox, filled the tin to the brim. Holding her breath, she gulped down the contents. After that, she barely had the strength or sense to crawl in under the pile of sougans before complete anaesthesia set in.

That's how Max found her, sometime about noon the next day. The spent storm, which already was showing signs of renewing itself, had washed away the great red puddle before the door so that Max missed it at first. He had been more concerned that the cabin was locked-up tighter than a bear's bowels in hibernation, and more than ever perturbed upon peering through the window, to see Marty lying abed. Then he saw the bullet hole, and was convinced she was dead. He went into the lean-to at the back of the cabin, removed the false pile of stovewood that hid his "other way" out of the cabin, "just in case of a sudden visit from a Federal Revenue man or a State Game Warden."

His first shock of disbelief came with the sound of Marty's raucous snoring and the smell of liquor on her breath. It didn't make sense; she had a revulsion against the stuff. Then he found his rifle on the floor. One cartridge exploded, one small hole in the windowpane! Furious, Max flung back the bars, unlocked the door, and stepped outside. Where the porch floor sagged, were still puddles of water, and in front of the door was a discolored puddle. On closer inspection there were faint smears of blood along the floor from door to steps.

Beyond the steps nothing was visible but mud, water, broken twigs, and limbs. Max was not satisfied. He tramped around the cabin to the window and peered in. He was a tall man, but the bullet hole in the windowpane was still a good foot above his head. Too high for a Cinnamon bear on his hind feet, or that crazy black panther the natives up in the

Ridge Country kept talking about. The only thing that would've stood as high as that hole in the windowpane would be a grizzly, and it was too late in the season for grizzlies.

That meant Marty had missed. Max wasn't pleased about that. Marty never missed. She never got buck fever; she never screamed nor ran nor asked him to save her from anything. She just planted her feet, raised her rifle, and shot to kill. Max had always admired that in Marty, but it also made him ill at ease because it so conformed with all the rest of her emotional pattern. She just bluntly stood, or sat, or laid indifferently in his arms, and accepted everything that fate, or he, forced upon her. So why did she miss last night?

Max widened his area of inspection; the dull, leaden sky, the broken limbs hanging from every Tamarack, Spruce and Cedar; Lodgepole pines down like matches by the dozens. In all, a damp, bleak Montana March day. Max wasn't a great brain, but if Marty shot and missed, then why the blood on the porch?

Without warning, from the nearest Lodgepole thicket, came a commotion to raise your back hair. It was Jasper, the black and tan hound. Jasper was Max's constant companion, whether logging, bootlegging, or poaching. The urgency in the dog's excited barking was Jasper's "dog language" for something immediate and significant, such as a treed mountain lion or an ambushed, wounded bear.

Max slipped and slithered in his eagerness to get back into the cabin and grab up the rifle. Once away from the mud of the immediate clearing about the cabin, and in the shelter of the trees, it was easier going on the wet leaves and needles; and Jasper was only two or three hundred yards into the pine growth.

The hound was standing at the end of a great hollow

Tamarack log which had fallen a century or two ago and had rotted out its heart for just such a refuge as it now was being used. Barely exposed, were the feet and ankles of a man.

With characteristic impulsiveness, Max put down his rifle, grasped the feet, and hauled away. What he expected to find, he didn't know, but hardly Oscar Fergusen, dead; shot through the abdomen, and with his life organs hanging out.

And a queer thing; Max dropped to his knees beside the corpse and peered bewildered. One of the nostrils was full of soil; not mud, but fine leaf mold, subsoil that you only find two or three feet down. His teeth and tongue were dirty, and there was sort of a paste of fine grit in his mouth as though it had been crammed full, and he hadn't been able to spit it all out; both of his ears were the same, and under his fingernails was this same silt; not the mud of last night's rainstorm; there were plenty of signs of that, too; his outer garments were plastered with wet and drying mud; especially one side on which he seemed to have pulled and dragged himself, because of the hole in his middle which kept him from standing upright.

One of his shoes had come off in Max's hand when he hauled him from the log, and Max had registered momentary surprise at the dry, fine, silty earth that had poured from the shoe. He pulled off the other shoe, and again it was inordinately full of dry leaf mold and rich, loamy earth. Now that he began to notice, there were other signs. Fergusen's overall pockets were full of this same earth; his shirt pocket—everywhere the rain had not reached showed evidence of fine, dry, silty earth. Even the gaping wound in the stomach was filthy with leaf mold; leaves, not mud! Loam and leaf mold!

Then there was another matter! Carefully, Max turned the body over; a small 30.06 hole showed where the bullet had entered his back; the big stomach wound was where the mushroom lead had burst through.

Max rose, wiped the mud off his knees with a blue bandana. Oscar Fergusen had been shot by a 30.06; had somehow wallowed in dry leaf mold clear up over his head; dragged himself to Max's cabin porch; and been refused entrance, and finally dragged himself up to the shelter of this hollow log to die. Max examined his rifle, dubiously. For Marty to have shot him with that one exploded shell, through that single clean hole in the upper frame of the window, Oscar would have had to stand on a three-foot ladder or else dangle from the roof, and obviously with his back to the cabin. So, just as obviously, that wasn't the answer.

Slowly Max returned to the cabin. Nothing more could happen to Oscar that Oscar would care about. Standing in the doorway, still in her rough cotton nightgown and bare feet, with a patched sougan about her shoulders, Marty, haggard and frowzy, still fusty and heavy with unspent sleep, waited.

Oscar Fergusen

In the whole of the northwestern section of the state of Montana there was scarcely anyone who wasn't a refugee; an escapee of one kind or another. Certainly this was especially true in Yaates Valley. Max and a half-hundred others of his ilk, up here in this far country, were rebels against over-civilization; against complicated living, pressures of over-population and an abundance of law and order.

The nearest neighbors were Olaf Jorgesen, ex-New York taxi driver, now fifteen years escaped from the traffic of Manhattan Island, and Merle Jorgesen, his wife, refugee from a stranded New York road show.

Further down along the Forest Service road were the Butterfield boys; refugees from prison records in Indiana. Up Salt Creek way was Jennie Loughner, a refugee from a Seattle call house. The Steinburgs (who ran the only gasoline pump from Mt. Baldy to Troy, a hundred and ten miles), were refugees from small college campus prejudice and intellectual snobbery. And finally, the Macklesons, with their fourteen children over on the Forks who had unsuccessfully run away from economic disaster. They'd been in the valley only three years, and in June the oldest girl, Velma, was fixed to become an unwed mother for a second time; as for Edna and Arlene, the second and third daughters, chastity no longer rested with them, either.

Oscar Fergusen, in his middle forties, came into the Yaates Valley seven years ago. Even then he was a gaunt, cadaverous man. The first moment Marty saw him, there was a flashing instant when she thought of her father. To put it another way, she hated him on sight. But this was nothing to her antagonism when rumor depicted Oscar Fergusen a wife deserter; a refugee from family life. One version had it that he had abandoned three children, a boy and two girls— another, that it was five, all girls—another said Fergusen had run off with a voluptuous redhead secretary, but what with kited checks and the authorities close on their heels, the girl fled and Fergusen had just made it across the line into the Montana back country.

This last was hardly realistic, inasmuch as Montana had all the paraphernalia of law enforcement, including con-scientious peace officers and extradition laws. But the natives doubted whether extradition laws really applied as far north and west in Montana as the Yaates. There was some reason for their feeling of immunity, perhaps. It was a long tortuous Forest Service road from the county seat. From early September to the end of the following May the road was either bogged down in mud, a running freshet of melting snow and rain water, or else choked off and impassable by ten feet of snow or a landslide. And always in the finest weather, Lodgepole pines fell across the road for no reason at all. No one traveled the Forest Service road without an axe and saw. The Valley was seventy miles by road from authority, but psychologically and factually, "an impossibly far-off place," and Yaaters were a queer lot who were best left to their own devices.

Except for the infrequent U.S. Forest Service man, an occasional Federal Revenue Agent, or a snoopy State Game Warden, peace officers were rarely seen, and never called upon.

Thus if the victims of Yaates Valley didn't die often or too spectacularly, and their deaths were reported over the Forest Service telephone in a decent, noncommittal, factual manner with something of a law-abiding air, further investigation was felt a waste of time. In truth, the valley would have resented it as intrusive and unfriendly.

The Sheriff, annoyed by the buzzing and crackling of the makeshift phone service, might say with perfunctory regret, "Too bad; he should have been more careful." The District Attorney's office was always grateful with, "Thanks for calling, but that seems to be outside our province," and the Coroner's office would probably add an admonition, "Well, don't let the body lie around, get it underground. Regulation six feet."

It was during her second year in the Valley that Marty had her first glimpse of Fergusen. And it was a full two years after that before Oscar Fergusen and Max had gone into their "poaching" venture. This had been justification on a few occasions for Oscar to be at the cabin for short moments and at odd hours. Nobody came up as far as Max's cabin much. Max didn't encourage it! Marty always went to the woodshed lean-to or out into the Lodgepole thicket when company was anticipated.

After that first momentary reminder of her father, the thought had been quickly thrust down into Marty's unconscious. On closer "inspection" there actually was no resemblance. But she never forgave him, and never saw the man's face that another bitter, secret drop of poison wasn't squeezed from her heart and left to fester in the dark, forbidding places of her soul.

The first time he came to the cabin when Max was away caught Marty unprepared. The violence of her emotions left her trembling, but she managed to slam the door on him and shoot the bolt. He hadn't said a word, there was no need; it was all plainly written in the greedy eyes. That time, he had left at once.

On the next surreptitious visit, he must have hung around the edge of the clearing until he was able to slip up on the porch between Marty and the doorway. That time, Marty escaped into the Lodgepole thicket.

It was two days before her nineteenth birthday, her fifth year in the Yaate, and on Oscar Fergusen's third attempt, that he crept in behind her and caught her fairly. It was a mid-March afternoon, and she'd been off guard in one of her "soft moments" as she stood on the river bank watching the first spring sunshine on the ripples.

She didn't fight. There was no resistance, just an indifferent limpness. But she did tell him that Max was due home from Bonner's Ferry sometime within the next two hours. Fergusen didn't believe her and, moreover, had no inclination of giving up what he'd waited so long to achieve. Then unexpectedly he sensed a new submissiveness in the girl, and he listened as she told him that the week following Max was making one of his long runs to Spokane. He was excited to hear her say that if he'd wait and come then, say on the twenty-first, there would be time enough for everything.

It was Marty's apparent eagerness to connive with him that intrigued his lust-fuddled mind and curbed his momentary instincts in favor of the larger, lustier adventure.

The clandestine proposal had come out of Marty as easily and naturally as though it had been thought out in detail and rehearsed. And yet she had had no pre-knowledge, no conscious hint that she would say and act in this prescribed manner. Still, she knew why she was doing it the moment the words were out of her mouth. It came to her as a revelation; a whole plan, complete in every detail. Deep in her unconscious it had been thought out and rehearsed; below the surface of realization, it had been long ready and waiting for fulfillment. Though it still may never have come to fruition if Fergusen had minded his own affairs and looked away from her.

Be Sure He's Dead

Max pushed past Marty in the doorway and went to the Forest Service telephone, put in the cabin of any Yaates man who agreed to fight fires in his area when called upon. It was an ancient wall affair with a bell crank. He took down the receiver and twisted the handle three times, the signal for the Outside operator. He picked up the stub of pencil hanging on a piece of dirty twine from the nail beside the art calendar, circled that day, twenty-second of March, and eyed with a flicker of humor and appreciation the sleek nude artist's model, spread on a silk and satin bed in abandon as she held a white French-type telephone receiver to her ear, obviously a gratuitous invitation to the whole masculine world. From the calendar, Max's eyes wandered to the window with the 30.06 hole in the pane, and a bleak and a noncommittal expression settled in them as he waited patiently for his connection.

Presently, the operator at the county seat answered from a long way off—thin, querulous and vague. She didn't know whether the Sheriff had returned from his South Dakota pheasant hunt...District Attorney?...No, it was his lunch hour, and he didn't have any phone where he was going...Yes, she supposed she might get the Coroner, which she finally did.

"This is Max...Yeah, Max Shoemaker, up in Yaates Valley. Tried to reach the Sheriff and the District Attorney, but no soap, so I'm giving it to you. Oscar Fergusen's dead of a gunshot wound...Yeah, probably self-inflicted when he tripped and fell, out looking for a little venison. Sure, I know this isn't venison season, but what're we supposed to eat, up here in the woods? Cows don't grow on bushes and bear meat's no good at this season, even if you could find one. Okay, we'll bury him. Just wanted you people down at the county seat to know about it first. Sure. . .Okay. . .'Bye!"

On his way out to get a shovel and pickaxe to throw on his truck, Max stopped to look at Marty for a moment, considering whether to say anything at all. Finally he said doubtfully, "He bother you much?"

Marty looked away and shook her head.

Max nodded. "Never try to bury a man or cook a bear until you're sure he's dead!" Satisfied that the subject was considered summed-up and closed, Max went out.

When he had loaded his tools and what remained of Oscar Fergusen onto his truck and driven away, Marty put on shoes without stockings, a bedraggled sweater, a skirt without underwear, and a heavy ankle-length mauve cloth coat, frayed at the hem, elbows, and buttonholes, and followed the path along the river back up into a small gully under a heavy clump of yew. Here in the loamy leaf mold and silt-soil Marty saw with her own eyes how the grave had burst open. Her own private resurrection! She'd only been able to bury him about two feet because at three feet she'd come to hardpan, and it had turned her shovel. Two feet seemed enough after the exertion of rolling the body in the hole, even though in his stupid hunger Fergusen had followed her instructions and come to the very edge of the open grave, where she had shot him from ambush.

PART V

Madame and Eve

August, 1940

Spider Creek was a far piece on foot up Yaates Valley, and the Larch and Tamarack-shaded dirt road to Jennie Loughner's Lodgepole cabin was as hot and dusty as it was crooked and stony.

Not nearly so crooked and stony, however, as the road Eve Corvell had fixed her mind to travel this hot August afternoon when she first turned her steps toward Jennie's.

Had the Widow Corvell suspected her daughter's intentions, she'd have sent Eve to her attic room in their one-room cabin instead of issuing ultimatums. Had Wayne Morgan known what was in Eve's mind, there would have been hell a-poppin' in all the primary colors. Not that Eve was undisciplined, only sixteen and desperate.

Since Eve had come of age, according to Yaates Valley thinking, Wayne had been pressing her to set a date for their marriage. Wayne had been showing his preference since Eve turned fifteen. Hal Morgan, his father, had expressed approval; and Ella Corvell had said jubilantly it was the one good thing to happen to the Corvells in the three years since Justan had died under his cot at the mill, leaving her a widow, and Eve fatherless.

Yaates Valley was entranced. It liked its brides young and beautiful, its bridegrooms lusty and eager. Wayne was as dark and handsome in his way as Eve was blonde and effervescent in hers. More than that he was a serious, hard-working abstemious, religious-minded boy. His father had a quarter section of the top haying land, another half section of virgin timber, and was prepared to deed a quarter section to Wayne and build him a first-class cabin, an oversized root cellar and a log barn that'd house six or eight head of stock through a Montana winter.

You know by this that Hal Morgan had more than his share of the meager wealth of the valley. But nobody begrudged him as he represented the backbone of neighborliness. No pretense of an education and never holding himself above the most indigent, he was always ready with a generous hand in any sort of misfortune.

When Eve tossed her sweet, gay head and laughed at Wayne's urgency, the citizens approved, for a girl as pretty and pert as Eve had every right to be as flirty and frivolous as she had a mind-to before she let herself be taken. It was part of a girl's heritage and showed an independence of spirit. "Folks" doubly enjoyed it because everyone felt assured that in good time Eve would submit, and Wayne would have his way.

But what intrigued the neighbors only roused impatience in Wayne. No young man has an overabundance of humor where his heart is involved. With Wayne it was worse because he was not light-minded and found no pleasure in dalliance. When he fished, he fished for meat, and a tricky, resolute trout only irritated him. When he went to buy a horse, he came with his money in his hand and any attempt at a dicker or a horse-trade threw him into a fury. Similarly with Eve, he wanted it cut and dried!

He complained to his father, and Hal went to see Ella Corvell. Eve's mother was in a panic. Since her husband's death they'd had exactly ten dollars a month from the mill's pension plan, and the idea of losing Wayne was unthinkable.

First she spoke to Eve as a reasoning mother, but when the girl shrugged lightly, she took a sharper tone. Eve was evasive; then out of fright the Widow Corvell spoke to her daughter in plain unvarnished Montana English. Eve, flushed and rebellious, flung herself out of the cabin and with premeditated vindictiveness took the long road up Spider Creek to Jennie Loughner's.

Jennie's Occupation

When Jennie retired from her Lake Union establishment at age forty-five, she was known in Seattle as a strict, decent-minded, conscientious Madame with a twenty-five-year reputation for the most respectable house in the entire Northwest. She had been born a farm girl, so when old Lincoln McCary, a twice-a-year client and one of the original settlers of Yaates Valley, died and willed her his Spider Creek homestead, she had accepted the gift, paid taxes on it and in due time retired into the Yaate, full of pungent memories, good deeds and an easy conscience.

No one had reason to complain. She was a pleasant neighbor and an asset to the valley. The women found her excellent company, and the men held her in slightly embarrassed but respectful awe. Nevertheless, though never said, it was tacitly understood that Yaate Valley girls of an impressionable age must not become too friendly in case some of Jennie's past just might rub off.

Her complete acceptance never became a problem as Jennie was tolerant of other people's prejudices. Besides, her cabin was ten miles from her nearest neighbor, and Jennie, while friendly, was neither pushy nor overly gregarious.

She had a gaunt brindle milk cow, a very gentle old off-white nag of a horse she rode on mail day, a ewe, two lambs, two milk goats, and ten Hampshire hens and a rooster with bedraggled tail feathers. Jennie was always saying she was going to put the rooster in the stewpot and get herself a cock with his tail feathers up and spread. She did like a male animal to have his tail feathers up. But don't misunderstand, Jennie was not rough-spoken. She carried herself with an air that set off her gray hair and gingham apron. There was a solid impression of self-sufficiency; of the pioneer woman; of our wagon train grandmothers.

Jennie Loughner was unlettered in the formal sense, but her knowledge was full, complete and endless in what a born farm woman should know. She could read, write, and cipher, certainly; but it was her uncomplicated simplicity, her innate goodness, and her refusal to compromise with wrong as she saw it, that defined her as a woman of character.

In the ordinary course of events she should have married and become the mother of a dozen stalwart sons. They would have had to be sons! There was that about Jennie which made men turn to her. That's why her house on Lake Union had such standards of excellence! She instinctively knew, in the deeper sense, why men came to a house of prostitution, and she imparted that warm, womanly, one almost might say, motherly knowledge to her girls.

In fact, before she accepted a new girl, she made certain the applicant could be molded to her philosophy.

Many were rejected after an initial interview. Jennie would not tolerate a foul mouth, a liar, a thief, nor a girl who had a grudge against the world, which invariably meant a grudge against men. She abhorred drunkenness and drug addiction. Physical daintiness was a fetish with her. A girl in the toils of a pimp or organized white slavers she sent packing, as she did one either actively or potentially a criminal, or had among her friends or acquaintances persons of low or unlawful tendencies.

If the candidate passed this first inspection she was sent to old Doctor Lincoln Malcom, not only for a clean bill of health, but general physical soundness, for it was Jennie's theory that a working girl must be a healthy young animal to be a satisfaction to herself and a gratification to the client.

After she qualified she was kept in the house under observation for a week. She was required to care for her own room, and it was inspected daily. She mingled with the other girls, ate at the common table and generally was given freedom of the house. If she was uncooperative, restive, moody, sulky, quick-tempered, or in any other manner vicious or undisciplined, she disappeared.

It was Jennie's belief that men were driven to a professional house out of frustration and loneliness; that the boy in every man was trying to recapture the comfort and momentary security of a mother's arms; the warmth of the maternal bosom; and that any girl with compassion and a little knowledge of the human heart could be a most welcome substitute. If she was soft and gentle, smelled nice and was responsive to the crying need of the moment, she became a haven—a nesting place—a sanctuary for an exhausted spirit. Thus a man's pain was lessened, and for a little while he was a man fulfilled.

At no time was the lewd, the perverse, nor the vicious acceptable either in her girls or in her clients; and this had been so long a tradition, it seldom had to be dealt with.

Jennie never for a moment let the girls forget they were fulfilling a wholesome and legitimate function in normal society. Above all, there was neither stigma nor dishonor in this oldest of professions. In her sincerity, she convinced the authorities and the community at large to such a degree that Jennie Loughner and her girls were tolerated all the years of Jennie's career. Not once had one of Jennie's girls ever been in jail. In the first place, she would no longer have been Jennie's girl; but more important, it demonstrated the quality of the girls Jennie selected and the amazing acceptance of her principles and philosophy. Over the years some of the girls left her to become wives and mothers. Jennie always credited her basic training for the high percentage of grateful husbands resulting from these marriages.

That was the background of the Jennie Loughner who now at forty-seven milked her brindle cow up on Spider Creek, chopped her own firewood, made butter and goat cheese, carded her own wool, and rode her off-white nag down to the Federal Building once a week on Friday mail day.

Yesterday had been mail day, and Jennie had been down to pick up her mail bag and a few items of dry groceries Zack Taylor had brought in on the mail truck. She'd heard the gossip of Wayne Morgan's pressing for a wedding day and Eve's dalliance. She'd caught sight of both. The valley called them a handsome pair and thought of them as the next thing to a storybook romance. The poor but beautiful heroine had caught the fancy of the rich man's handsome son.

To Jennie there was no truth in it. Perhaps that was why Wayne and Eve were in her mind as she went down into her blueberry patch below the garden.

As Jennie Saw Them

The sun was warm on her back, and the berries were a delight to her eye in their crisp purple lusciousness amongst the cool green leaves.

She thought that Eve Corvell was beautiful only because she was young. Behind that sixteen-year-old's effervescence there was a hard, self-centered little personality that was going to give a husband a bad time. She would make no man a satisfactory wife, and during her years in Seattle Jennie had turned away scores of Eves from her house. They essentially were selfish, grasping, and in the end became discontented and martyrs. They left clients unsatisfied and therefore disgruntled; guilt-ridden for having imposed on an unwilling girl.

Jennie's pail was half-filled when she came to consider Wayne. She frowned! Wayne disturbed her deeply.

Yaaters called him handsome, manly, hardworking, reserved, more religious than makes most young folks comfortable, and chaste beyond their understanding. This last was one of the excitements of the romance. Too few Yaates girls arrived at the altar completely whole, and certainly no young man. But in the case of Eve and Wayne this was rumored not to be so.

Jennie conceded to Wayne a good nose, a wide brow, and a fine head of hair; also that he was romantically rugged. His looks didn't hide from her, however, the sensuous mouth, the chin that didn't jut out equal with the rest of his features, nor the too-hot eyes. Yaates' girls called them mysterious, haunting. Jennie called them haunted, and they hid no mysteries from her.

He was manly beyond his age only because he controlled himself with an impossibly tight checkrein. He was hard-working because he was driven to a frenzy of physical activity by terrible compulsions. He was reserved because of a fearful inner conflict that he struggled to keep within the confines of his secret self; he was religious because he was frantically seeking a relief never found; and if he was chaste it was only in the flesh. In this abstemious prudery, and the cause behind it, was the core of his unnatural stoicism.

In Jennie's experience she had never questioned "why men are as they are" only understanding "how they are." And she saw in Wayne a dangerous young man. She also knew from experience nothing was to be done. She could no more warn Eve against Wayne's complexity than she could warn Wayne against Eve.

She was still on her knees in the berry patch when Eve came around the corner of the cabin. It was a weary, footworn girl, hot with the exertion of the last stony uphill mile, who stood uncertain now she was here. She'd come in desperation, but much of the grievous anger had subsided with her spent energy. Suddenly she was not nearly so sure why she was here.

Jennie saw her at once, and rising with her now-full pail, came to greet her.

"You're Ella Corvell's girl!" she said in surprise, feeling that in some inexplicable manner her thoughts had material-ized the girl. Seeing Eve's exhaustion, she exclaimed, "You ambled all the way up here on shanks' mares? You poor tyke!" And taking Eve's arm she bustled her into the cabin, sat her down, ordered her to take off her shoes, and poured out a big glass of cool, creamy-rich milk.

"Gracious sakes," she worried, picking up Eve's discarded sandals and dusting them off with her apron, "What brung a snip of a girl wanderin' way up Spider Creek, for pity's sake?"

Eve looked at her mutely. Jennie recognized the girl was not fit to talk so she breezed on in a friendly, neighborly chatter:

"I'm aiming to put up maybe twenty, thirty pints of blueberries for winter pies and still have enough for preserves and jam with scads left over. Suppose your mother could use any blueberries?"

A flicker of a smile crossed Eve's face.

"Another thing, my ten hens are lining up like hungry cats, waiting their turn to get on the nest these days, so I've got fresh eggs galore. I've put down twenty dozen in water glass already, and I can spare three, four dozen easy as not if Mrs. Corvell can use them. Though, Lord knows how you're going to get home on foot with a bucket of blueberries and four dozen eggs." She laughed at the idea. Then more reasonably, "Tell you what, I'll ride them down on Whitey come mail day."

She wrung out a towel in cold water and handed it to Eve.

"Here, wipe off your face and arms with this cold towel. See how refreshed you'll feel."

Eve set down her empty glass and did as she was told.

Jennie put two heaping spoons of spider-leg tea in a big, brown pot and poured in boiling water from a teakettle off the woodstove. A pungent aroma filled the cabin as she brought the pot and two cups to a small homemade table beside her own chair and made herself cozy.

"Goodness, child," she said, eyeing the girl, "you've growed into a woman this past year." Eve flushed and looked away.

Jennie nodded. "I thought so yesterday, mail day, when I glimpsed you down at the Federal Building."

Eve nodded. "I saw you," she said simply. "Maybe that was why I was put into a mind to come and see you."

"Oh?" Jennie poured out the tea and handed a cup to Eve. "Milk for strength; tea for courage," she said with a friendly wink.

The tea not only revived Eve's spirits but her resentments, and presently Jennie was being acquainted not only with the girl's rebellion at being pushed into a marriage she wasn't ready for, with a man for whom she had no love; but worst of all, seeing a situation upon her from which there was no escape. She hated the Yaate; always had!

A few times she'd been Outside, of course, but no farther than the county seat. That was not the world she dreamed of, either. But the high droning of the Danish Transworld Airliner from Los Angeles across the North Pole to Europe which passed directly over the Yaate twice a week, was! So was the world symbolized by the queer foreign stamps and the undecipherable handwriting on the letters the Gruenwalds received in their weekly mail sacks.

She hoarded an old mutilated copy of *National Geographic* magazine which she'd seen fall from Max Shoemaker's logging truck, and which she'd rescued. It was all about Paris, France, with wonderful advertising of ships to travel on, trains, other airlines, fine hotels and exciting displays of exotic foods, clothes and cosmetics.

She'd shown the magazine to Wayne just once. After flipping through a few pages he'd tossed it aside to tell her about the Jackson Fork that had broken down that afternoon with still forty acres of hay in the shock.

She'd tried to talk to the valley girls her own age about the Outland, but they wanted to talk about the Yaates boys, about getting married, guess who was the father of Louise Ackerman's baby coming next month, and the Ridge girls the Yaates boys went to see on Saturday nights.

Eve, breathless now with the flood of her bitterness, at last came to her mother's edict and let her tale come to its inevitable conclusion: how she'd been told plainly that unless she married Wayne Morgan, and at once, she could get out and make her own bed and find out what a hard, comfortless bed it could be.

When she'd finished Jennie said a surprising thing, "Do you believe in God?"

Eve looked disconcerted at the unexpected question but answered without hestitation, "Of course."

Jennie nodded. "Then you must believe that if you pray to Him, He'll find a way to help you."

Eve was slower in her response this time. A bit of the rebel began to show around her mouth.

"However," said Jennie encouragingly, "God helps those who help themselves."

"I thought that's what I was doing when I came to you."

Jennie laughed. "Well, me and God are old acquaintances," said Jennie, "more than most citizens suppose.

However, I ain't so sure I'm the answer to a young girl's prayer."

She looked at Eve thoughtfully for perhaps three seconds: "Just what did you have in mind?"

Eve held her eyes for a fraction of a moment, then flushed, and her glance slid away.

"That's what I thought," said Jennie tartly. "You said to yourself, 'Jennie Loughner's an old experienced Madame.' You thought, 'I'm pretty and young, and that's all I've got for to make my way in the world. Jennie can tell me how to use what I've got better'n anybody else in the valley.'"

Eve defiantly lifted her chin.

"Look, Deary, you can't bear the idea of giving yourself up to a young man you've known from a little girl. You think you're going to like a stranger any better?"

Eve's eyes blazed. "Wayne Morgan can have me right tonight if he'd pay me enough to get out of the Yaate. It's not giving that means anything; it's being tied to him forever and ever; trapped here the rest of my life."

"You don't know what you're talking about."

"I know what I want."

"No sixteen-year-old girl knows what she wants."

"You know what I'm going to do if you don't help me?" Eve said dangerously.

"No," Jennie answered gently, "No, I don't!"

"I'm going up on the Ridge. The girls up there get money every Saturday night. Men come from all over the

Kootney Country, even from as far as Kalispell."

"You'll get a lot more than money, you go up there," warned Jennie grimly.

Eve looked stubborn!

"That Ridge is the dregs and shame of humankind, and no girl that goes up on the Ridge ever comes down on account she ain't fit for any place else."

"I'm not going to stay here and marry Wayne Morgan."

"And in all my born days, I never helped an innocent girl into the profession," Jennie's mouth was set. "It always did go against everything that's decent in me, and it always will."

"You were a Madame for twenty-five years!" Eve's voice was flat and brash.

Jennie nodded unperturbed.

"And before that, what were you?"

Jennie's eyes lighted with tolerant amusement. "You really are a scratchy little cat once you get your claws unsheathed, ain't you?"

"Well?" persisted Eve.

"Why, yes," agreed Jennie amiably, "it's just like any other profession, you've got to start at the bottom."

"Is it any worse for me than for you?"

Jennie stared into the bottom of her empty teacup for a few moments, and then looked at Eve with serious, honest eyes.

"I'm going to tell you a story. I expect it ain't going to do either of us any good, but it just might, so I'm going to tell it."

She whisked the dregs about in the bottom of her cup for a moment, and then began. "When I was seventeen," she said, "I fell in love with a young man my pa hated. Pa was a small, unsuccessful rancher in eastern Oregon, and I was born and raised a ranch girl. I never knew my father when he wasn't mad at something; eastern Oregon, the climate, the stony soil, but mostly he hated his neighbors. The boy I loved was one of them neighbors, and Pa hated him more than most because he was making a living while Pa was going broke. Fritz was Swiss, and Pa also hated foreigners.

"Well, I ran off across the state line to Nevada, married Fritz, and I was happy. I knew right off I was going to like married life. I got pregnant during our two weeks' honeymoon.

"The day we come back to Fritz's ranch Pa came over with his rifle. Fritz saw him coming and got down his deer gun. I begged him not to do it, but he went out to meet Pa, and the minute he stepped outside, Pa fired and Fritz fired back. Pa was shot through the heart, but Fritz lived long enough to say 'goodbye.'"

Jennie looked out of the corner of her eye to see what impression she was making. In her interest Eve had momentarily forgotten her own grievance. This much of Jennie's autobiography had been recalled in a dry, matter-of-fact, impersonal voice as though of no great concern.

"Well, I went over to our ranch to tell my mother, but she wouldn't talk to me. She just said, 'Get out, you slut,' and slammed the door in my face."

Jennie's face was still placid. Eve, appalled, hardly breathed.

"That same night I took what little money was left from the honeymoon and got on a bus for Portland. When Fritz's place was sold and the mortgages all paid and a Pendleton attorney had taken his fees, there was about $300 left. It was sufficient until my baby was born. So there I was in Portland, no money, a baby, and myself to feed and shelter.

"One night when I'd been out of money for about a week and was in so desperate a frame of mind I didn't know what way to turn, I got down on my knees and prayed. I put my whole heart into it.

"I felt better right away. When I got up on my feet I knew everything was going to be all right. I took my baby son down to my landlady's apartment; she'd helped me with him several times before. I went out on the street and began to walk. Nothing happened, but I knew as sure as I was Jennie Loughner that my prayer was going to be answered.

"I'd been walking steady, maybe two hours, when I came to a city park with benches, and I sat down to rest my feet. My feet and legs were used to pasture land and orchard soil, and the pavement made them burn and feel swollen. Besides one of my shoes was pinching my little toe something awful, so I took off my shoe to ease the pain.

"All at once a girl came out of the shadows and sat beside me. I don't know, maybe she'd been watching me; I'd been too taken with my aching feet and wondering how my prayer was going to be answered to notice.

"Well, the long and short of it was that she seemed to want to talk, and before I knew it I was telling her about being a farm girl alone in the city with a new baby and needing money. I didn't say anything about the praying. I just said I needed money and was out walking the streets to get some. She said so was she, and if I wanted to tag along she thought she could fix it up for both of us.

"I know now that she misunderstood what I said about walking the streets, just as I had no idea what she had in mind. I didn't know a streetwalker from Adam's Off Ox, but I did know right then and there that God had answered my prayer. I put on my shoe, my feet didn't hurt any more, and we did get money.

"I was pretty shocked and panicky when I understood what we were about, but I took a grip on myself and reasoned it out. 'Jennie Loughner,' I said, 'you asked God to show you the way to take care of yourself and your baby, and he's showed you! So if it's all right with God, then it's got to be all right with you.'

"I felt better about it, too, the minute I got to talking with the young fellow that selected me. He was even more lonesome and out of place in the city than I was. He'd come from a ranch down in southern Oregon, near Phoenix, and this was his first job away from home; and my, how he did hanker after the ranch, the stock, and the big farm breakfasts his ma used to cook. Restaurant flapjacks were tough and soggy, the ham tasted phony, the eggs small and not very fresh, and the cream wasn't as rich as whole milk back home.

"But most of all he hadn't been close to a woman since leaving home. He was used to three sisters and a grandmother besides his mother, and it haunted him day and night how fresh, wholesome, and sweet they seemed in retrospect. He kept smelling my hair and saying how it reminded him of his mother when he was a little boy.

"Well, you know, I could hardly bear to take his money, but he seemed to want to give it, and I needed it so desperately. You know, that was the kind of experience I had over and over again there in Portland. After a while I got a new idea about men and why they paid money for a woman's company, and it's stuck with me all my life.

"Not that there aren't mean men, but there are mean girls, too. I always say most of the meanness and ugly things that come out of men are invited by girls. They seem to feel dirty and put upon, the victims of men's passions, and they take their revenge in getting as much money as they can and giving as little as they dare in return. I thought a lot about this and begun to think how much happier everybody'd be if the girls could understand about the good they were doing. Somehow I got it fixed in my head that I could thank the Good Lord for answering my prayer when I was so desperate by having a house of my own and teaching the girls the true meaning of their calling. That's how I come to start fresh in Seattle with a place of my own.

"And, you know, I never did find a man who wasn't looking for tenderness more than he was for lustfulness when he got right down to the reason for coming to my place. No matter how rough or blustering or hard he was in the beginning, somewhere lurking around the edges was the little boy looking for mother comfort. When a girl can find that in a man, whether he's old enough to be her grandfather or young enough to be her son, well, I just defy anyone to find anything terrible about it."

Eve had been listening with a growing look of confusion on her face. The sight of it broke Jennie's preoccupation.

"It's like any other profession," she said looking at Eve thoughtfully. "You put your heart and soul, your best effort in it and something pretty wonderful's bound to take place, and everyone is rewarded. Is it better for a girl to feel cheap, misused and dishonored, or for her to feel there is a great, good purpose to what she's doing? Actually, she is the human expression of Mother Nature herself, closer to men's fundamental needs even than his wife; more accessible than his natural mother; in fact, she is in a sense the universal mother of mankind."

There was something of a mocking look in Eve's eyes.

"Nobody in the Yaate thinks the Ridge girls are being little mothers; least of all the boys who go up there Saturday nights."

Jennie nodded, "They're the poor, ignorant girls I was talking about; riddled with bad habits; feeling ashamed and hating themselves for what they're doing. I don't hold any truck with that kind. I'd be the first to say, 'wipe them from the face of the earth.'"

Jennie looked at Eve ruefully and thought to herself, "Now looky what I've done. Broke a rule I laid down for myself when I first come into the Yaate! Not to rub folks' noses in my past. So here I dig up the whole blessed mess, and for what? A spit of a girl with no more idea what I've been talking about than Sanskrit, whatever that is! She don't have the big heart for it, just as I thought."

The sun which had been laying a rich golden runner through the open door and across the uncarpeted floor suddenly dipped behind a distant peak, and Spider Creek was transformed into a soft purple paradise with only the tallest treetops still a glitter of yellow. Just as quickly, the heat of the high mountain afternoon gave way to the cool of evening presaging a frosty northern Montana night.

The cabin was at once melancholy with shadows. Jennie came to her senses.

"Land sakes, look what time it is," she said starting up. "You got to get started back for home."

Eve didn't move. She looked stubbornly adamant.

"Now, come child," urged Jennie, "nobody knows where you are, and if you ain't home in decent time Lord knows what your mother'll do."

"She told me to get out and make my own bed."

"Well, you ain't gonna make it in my cabin," Jennie assured her. "People find you spent the night with Jennie Loughner, and they're going to think the worst about you, and they just might ride me out of the Yaate on a rail."

"I might have known you wouldn't help."

There was so much hard, young bitter resentfulness in Eve as she stood up that Jennie hesitated.

"Is it because I'm a virgin?" demanded Eve.

"No girl's fit for the profession before she's had a good twenty years of solid trouble."

Eve's face darkened.

Jennie studied her for a long moment. Finally she came to a decision.

"Come on out and help me gather the eggs and feed the stock."

Eve followed her without a word.

Milking the Goat

There were seven large brown eggs in the nests, and the hens fluttered and squawked happily over their feeding of grain and table scraps. The bedraggled old rooster clucked and raised a ruckus over each newly discovered tidbit. Jennie eyed him with disfavor. "The minute I can lay hands on a young squirt who prides himself on his tail feathers, the stewpot for you," she promised ominously.

The high bleat of the goats and soft baaing of the sheep called them to the barnyard, and in a few minutes all the stock had its separate pitchfork of hay. The dried mountain grass and clover mixed with alfalfa smelled as pungent as a freshly opened packet of tea leaves, and all about the whole scene was the restful mystic beauty of a Millet painting.

Jennie made no further reference to Eve or her problem. She led one of the goats up onto its raised stanchion so she could milk while standing. The goat's udder was distended, glutted with milk until the blue veins stood out in relief, the teats full and erect.

There was so much earthy pleasure in Jennie's appreciation of this simple farm chore and such gratefulness from the goat on being relieved of her burden of milk, the two seemed attuned in a homey natural way. Eve caught some of this abundance of graciousness and was contented to wait and watch.

It wasn't until the second goat had been brought to the

station that Jennie spoke. "You ever stop to think, the world outside's full of other kinds of women's work?" she asked without interrupting the rhythmic streams of milk.

"How would I know about anything?" Eve's words were not resentful now; only defeated. "What does any Yaater know? Nobody ever leaves the valley, or if he does he comes hurrying back like a rabbit scampering for the underbrush."

"It's pretty nice up here."

"I hate it."

"I can tell you one Yaater who's doing what he wants to do on the Outside.

"Who?"

"Marvin Culbertson! You remember him?"

Eve remembered vaguely. Marvin was Granny Culbertson's boy up on Salt Creek. He'd gone out of the valley when she was thirteen, to study medicine in Missoula.

"I hear tell he's coming home. He's run short of money, and quitting school for a spell to come back and take his old job at the sawmill to work up a new grubstake."

"He's educated." Eve dismissed Marvin as a once-in-a-lifetime phenomenon, distant and disassociated from her world.

"If a Yaates boy can get to be a doctor, why couldn't you get to be a nurse, if you set your mind to it?"

Eve looked at the older woman as though she were out of her senses.

"I know for a fact that nurses get good money and more than that, they get a chance to travel anywhere in the world. They need nurses bad, every place."

The second goat dispatched, Jennie released the animal with an affectionate pat, carried the pail of goat milk to the root cellar, strained it into a large crock and covered it with a fresh dish towel. She next took up a shiny three-gallon pail and went to where Old Brindle was eye-deep in her evening hay. Jennie made herself comfortable on a one-legged stool, gripped the pail between her knees, and tucking her head in bossy's flank began to draw off the milk with long practiced strokes that made the bottom of the pail sing, the milk to froth and foam.

"You know what I'd do if I was a young girl and wanted my independence? I'd write to Marvin and ask him about nursing, and then when he come home, I'd have a talk with him."

"It would take years, even if I could do it." Eve was restless and impatient. She couldn't picture herself with so much education; she couldn't even picture a nurse. She'd never seen one any more than she'd seen a duchess. They were all just impossible Outlanders in an inaccessible world.

"Tell you what," proposed Jennie, stripping the last of the milk from the left hind teat and the right fore one, then shifting to the opposite corners of the udder, "before you make any desperate resolves, I want you should do two things for me. Write to Marvin, for one. The other is to get down on your knees every night for a week and pray; that's the most important! And I mean pray like you meant it."

"Can I stay here?"

"No."

"Why?"

"I told you why, already."

"I can't go back home without saying I'll marry Wayne. My mother told me that."

"She'll give you a week, won't she?"

Eve gave this reluctant consideration.

"You ask me," Jennie predicted, "she'll be so happy to think you're reconsidering, she'll treat you like the returned Prodigal."

"And if nothing happens in a week?"

"Now ain't that a nice way to approach prayer! No wonder folks get so little help from the Lord!" In her indignation she gave such a violent tug on the teats that Brindle kicked out resentfully. "Soo, bossy...Soo...Soo," she said comfortingly. "That was my fault, and I apologize." She released one of the teats to soothe the cow's flank.

Eve's Big Gesture

That following Friday mail day Eve had complied with Jennie's first request. In the outgoing mail sack that Zack Taylor tossed into the back of his mail truck was a postcard to Marvin Culbertson.

Eve and her mother had walked the two dusty miles to the Federal Building in midmorning where the majority of Yaaters were gathered, enjoying the gossipy holiday mood that always characterized mail day.

Eve had put aside her stormy moodiness of the past few days and was the pert, ebullient, loquacious school girl familiar to Yaaters. She was quickly assimilated among the dozen others girls of her own age who segregated themselves from their elders at the picnic tables in the clearing between the Federal Building and the Forest Service road. Tittering, shrieks of inane laughter and a babble of young voices came up to the elders.

"Convention of blue jays," Romeo McFeddor called them.

The center of the girls' interest was divided between Eve, when she was going to marry Wayne, and Louise Ackerman, who was eight months with child and refused to name the father. An Outlander would have found it hard to see in Louise a betrayed young woman in the girl's complacency and in her companions' light acceptance of her complications. In fact, most of the hilarity was coming from

131

a variety of outrageous speculations.

Edna Winters suggested Romeo McFeddor. There were shrieks of laughter, and Louise was as convulsed as the rest. Someone else thought it was Yaate's elder statesman, Seth Bascomb, who hadn't had a woman in the valley's memory, and Louise laughed until tears came. Then Eve guessed Hodge Sweeney's boy, Bert, who was barely twelve and had a cleft palate.

Louise shrieked, "Aw, now the secret's out," and all the girls whooped with delight. The mention of Bert Sweeney reminded Jay Hepple that her brother Guy, fourteen, had run away with the older boys up to the Ridge last Saturday night, and her father had taken a horsewhip to him when he came home. The girls were momentarily silent, eager for details.

"Guy said it was worth a whipping every Saturday night. He said what went on up on the Ridge would set a man's sougans on fire."

The girls giggled uncertainly, titillated, but a little at a loss.

"Is that all he said?" Eve demanded.

Jay shrugged.

"Except that a man could get more for two dollars up there than two dollars would buy anywhere else in the whole United States."

"Two dollars?" There was shocked disillusion in Eve's voice.

"Well, Guy doesn't get hold of two dollars once a year, so he's got a long wait for his next horsewhipping."

This struck the girls as hilariously funny. Only Eve continued to look thoughtful and sober. Suddenly Louise nudged her.

"There he comes."

Eve looked with the others. It was Wayne, dismounting from his cow pony at the hitching rack. He didn't even glance toward the picnic ground but strode stiffly withdrawn toward the crowd around the steps of the Federal Building. This was the first time Eve had glimpsed him since her visit to Spider Creek.

"You were born lucky, Eve Corvell," said Edna enviously, and all the girls showed signs of agreeing. In fact, Wayne did look favored above most of the Yaate's young men. His dark, serious face with its air of mystery and reserve was bound to give any lightminded girl pause.

"When are you going to set the wedding day?" Louise asked.

"Let him wait," said Eve lightly.

"My mother says there's a time for playing a fish and a time for landing him." Gracie Jorgeson was disapproving.

"If you don't want him, I'm next," Frieda Park announced.

The girls all looked at Eve, but she only laughed.

"My brother says he's either a virgin or cut," Louise couldn't help saying out of spite.

Eve flushed deeply, but recovered herself before the explosion of laughter had subsided.

When Wayne came back to the hitching rack with the Morgans' mail bag, she detached herself from the gathering and went to him as he was fastening the tie rope to the saddle.

"Were you leaving without even saying hello?" she asked.

Wayne surveyed her with smoldering eyes. "Yes," he said.

"Oh." There was so much relief in Eve's voice Wayne's face darkened. "Then you've stopped wanting to marry me?" Maybe this was what Jennie meant about an answer to her prayer. For a moment she'd forgot that she hadn't once been on her knees. She just couldn't bring herself to it.

"Eve, I want you should stop playing me." Wayne said tightly. "I'm in no frame of mind for it. Your ma told my pa that come Sunday you'd set the date. I'll see you Sunday." He swung himself up on the pony.

"I won't be at the Meeting House."

"Then I'll come over to your place."

"No," said Eve, "I'll meet you at the Spider Creek Forks tonight."

"What for?"

Eve shrugged, "Why put off what I've already made up my mind to."

Wayne sat still in his saddle looking down at the girl somberly, and then a smile of satisfaction lighted his face.

"I'll be there," he said.

"Don't say anything to anyone."

"Hardly!" He nodded and turned the pony, spurring the animal to a canter. There was about him the air of a man who'd completed a difficult deal and had come off best.

On the steps of the Federal Building Ella Corvell had been watching with relief. She said to Seth Bascomb with complacency, "It won't be long now."

Romeo McFeddor sitting on the steps at her feet with his skinning knife a-whittling a stick, looked out toward Mt. Baldy with a wolfish grin and said to no one in particular, "Ain't mothers Hell!"

Mrs. Corvell gave him a dirty look and went to join the Colemans with whom she and Eve were sharing a basket lunch.

Seth waited until she was out of earshot and then said to Romeo, "Sometimes, McFeddor, I swear to God, I don't know why the Earth don't swallow you up, unless it just plain couldn't stomach you."

Romeo grinned, yawned, and went back to whittling.

PART VI

Don't Whup Your Poppa

"Cripes in the High Corn," Romeo McFeddor said disapprovingly, as Junius Yarboro cuffed and pummeled his eldest boy, Sim, driving him around the corner of the Federal Building for further fisting. "The way Old Man Yarboro dusts them kids of his'n, you'd think he was a bull goose a-fightin' his way out of a pen of varmits."

"It ain't that Junius is a mean man," said the ancient Seth Bascomb worrying his frosted walrus mustache, "and it ain't that his whelps is any more frolicksome than any others. All young critters is ornery at various ages." Seth and Romeo sat on the steps of Bascomb's log house, known up and down the Valley as the Federal Building, it being the last stop of the weekly mail truck and the nearest thing to a post office the Valley afforded.

Romeo bit off a twist from an unsanitary plug of Old Ugly Twist and shoved the remainder back in his hip pocket along with an equally disreputable red bandana. "I make it," he surmised, "that Junius' stump ranch won't grow bread, even if he wasn't too lazy to plant it. So many kids and too many notches pulled up in his belt makes him a speck resentful."

"He ain't a mean man in general," Bascomb repeated,

adding reluctantly, "though he shouldn't ought to clean his plow as often as he does." And then defensively, "But young'ns is always cuttin' a big gut to bring a parent to the outer rim of shame and drink. Look at Case Hooper's boy! Down ridin' roughshod on them feisty Shadow Crik blisters; not one of 'em over ten, eleven, and yet you'd think they was Beelzebub's own Chippy Delight in Ram-Cat Alley! And so now Case Hooper's boy, Elmer's come bad and Case is out to round up a posse to ride up Shadow Crik and burn out the whole blamed forked-plague, mother and daughter, and drive them up on the Ridge to the cat-house settlement."

Romeo spat and nodded. "But he won't do it."

"Not with Doc Marvin takin' care of Elmer's canker," Seth agreed. "Still you can't blame a man for wantin' to burn down the fences of hell and stomp out the fire. Which only goes to show that *all* the blame ain't on Junius Yarboro. Offspring, 'specially when not wanted, can be pure poison to a man's peace of mind."

Romeo agreed heartily, eyeing a flock of young teenage girls arriving together from the Yaates school, some distance down the Forest Service road. "Looky yonder," he interjected. "Not a harmless one among 'em. Looky at 'em! Combs up and showy as a red flag! Every one of 'em pruney and ready for rimming!" He snorted, "Ha! On closer observation I'd be obliged to say them two split-tails in front already've been crimped up in the peach orchid, and the seeds' took root in fertile soil. Both of 'em chuffy to boulden in the place where a female gits chuffy to boulden on such occasions."

Seth Bascomb shook his head sadly. "You and me sit here, gab-fest and tickle our genitals with our eyes and imaginations, then go home to our vittles with good appetite, but what do you make of their kin folk? I swear, Romeo, I'd as soon see my box acomin' in on the next mail truck, as to face chick or child born of my seed."

Romeo cocked his ear. From around the corner of the Federal Building there came a garble of angry, muffled voices, thumps, and breathless exclamations of pain, fear, and brutal anger. Romeo listened for a long minute and shook his head.

"Well, it's in my mind that Junius shouldn't ought to fist his litter the way he does. That ain't no way to disencourage a young disposition." Romeo shifted his cud to make a pronouncement, "'Specially not Sim. That there boy's agettin' on toward sixteen and he's mighty near as big as Junius and strong as a young bull in full seed. Some day he's liable to turn on his old man and whale the bejesus out of him and who's to blame him?"

It was a year after this that Sim Yarboro quit the Yaates and went to shifting for himself. He drifted out of Montana, across the Idaho panhandle and into the Washington wheat fields, and from there down into Bend, Oregon, where he did handy jobs in a tourist camp one summer. The next the Yaates heard he was eating smoke with the firefighters at Crater Lake.

He seemed to be drifting aimless. About once a year we would hear he had ciphered out and was amblin' off somewhere else. We heard he worked the Redwood lumber camps in northern California and was a deckhand on a lumber schooner out of Tacoma for San Francisco. Then he was caught up in the draft and next the Valley heard was that Sim was a paratrooper in some foreign place.

He never once came home and nobody was surprised

because it was common talk what a miserable time old man Yarboro had given him. Junius let up somewhat on the younger kids after Sim migrated. Whether Sim's leaving brought him to his senses, whether he was getting along and didn't have the old fire any more, or whether his resentment against his young was centered in Sim, nobody could figure.

Sim was the firstling and some say that at times a jealous man just can't chamber a first-born son on account he still has a lot of seed to sow with a young wife, and another male, even smaller than an average salmon, is too much rivalry.

Whatsomever, for a breathing space the atmosphere around the Yarboro stump ranch cleared up considerably. When Sim had been gone for five or six years his two sisters, thirteen and fifteen, began to poot out in the middle and give signs of little people in the offing. Junius shrugged weary shoulders and said, "When they're big enough they're old enough—it's pure nature, and a father's a fool to buck it." But Mrs. Yarboro sickened even though the Reverend Mr. Grocer, on his spring circuit ride into the Valley, blessed the girls with reluctant husbands and sheepish fathers-to-be, both boys being still in their middle teens.

Then, to bend the stick until it broke, Sim's two brothers made it unanimous by shaking off the home lice to work for the P&X sawmill. The Yarboro stump ranch, never a paradise of tender affections nor a thing of beauty, now resembled the slum side of hell, deserted by everything but the grey phantom rats of discouragement and loneliness which gnawed away continuously at the last remnants of hope.

In this state of brutal misery Junius forced on Sim's mother a sixth pregnancy, but having already filled her so full of loathing hatred for having made a drifter out of

Sim, provoking his daughters to willfulness and wantonness, and having driven off the two younger boys, she came sour in her womb and crimped up on the porch. When Junius found her she had some way cooned into bed and pulled the coverlid up over her head. She must have suffered something wonderful before Seth Bascomb arrived and named her dead.

The midwife hailed from the Ridge to make her ready for her box reported Mrs. Yarboro had curdled the baby inside her and took it with her to spite Junius. Seth said midwives were next things to witches and lied out of malicious mischief. However, he did not say that he had found the rusty hat pin which had caused a shocking case of septicemia.

After Sim had been inducted it was as though the Army had gobbled him up. Nothing was heard for going on two years, until one mail day at the Federal Building, his older sister Martha passed the word that he was in a military hospital in San Francisco. What had brought him to this state was a mystery. The how, where, why, and the extent of his injury never did reach the Valley. Then there came word Sim was out of the hospital and was going to the University of California on the G. I. Bill, studying forestry and playing on the college football team.

"That there's like teaching a hungry fox pup to eat chickens," Seth Bascomb commented. "What in Chiny c'n a Californy school teach a Montana boy about trees?"

The Reverend Mr. Grocer thought perhaps it would make Sim eligible for a Federal appointment to the Forestry Service.

Romeo bit off a quid of Old Ugly and vouchsafed, "Takes a lot of play practice most like to teach a boy how to git in an' out of them purty store clothes that keeps them Federal boys proud and happy. 'N' don't forgit they gotta' learn how to chase them bugs with butterfly nets for the experimental station; likewise there's a special kind of pussyfootin' to be done on natives hereabouts who might be cuttin' forest timber or grazin' a few head of stock on government land."

"What's this here football business?" Seth wanted to know. "I hear it on the raaaadio but it's whoopin' and hollerin' and altogether senseless, seems like."

"That's college," explained Romeo.

"What is?"

"Whoopin', hollerin' and senseless."

"Don't seem like college is the thing Sim should be doin' right at the moment, with his ma alayin' cold and stiff in her box and the Reverend Mr. Grocer come in special to do the right thing." Seth lifted his old eyes to the circuit rider for confirmation.

"He's been gone a right long time, apparently without intention ever to communicate with his family or return to the Valley," the minister said gravely. "However, I took it upon myself to send a telegram to him in care of the university. That was three days ago and I've heard nothing. I have delayed too long now. If nothing is heard by today's mail truck, the services must go forward tomorrow morning without him."

The mail truck brought nothing from Sim. And no one actually had expected it. On the following morning, a Saturday, under the benign ministrations of the good Reverend, Mrs. Yarboro—Anna Daisy Phyllis Jeffery Yarboro—was buried in the presence of a hundred and sixty-seven Yaaters including Junius, her two younger sons, her two daughters and their husbands. All the

Yaaters could do for the late mother of Sim was done, except give her the final consolation with the presence of her favorite child.

World by the Tail

It was a considerable shock to folks when Sim rode in on the following Friday mail day with Zack Taylor and his mail truck from the county seat. To be quite honest, nobody knew who he was, when Sim climbed down from beside Zack and limped around to shake hands with Seth.

He was six foot one or two and a good two hundred and twenty pounds. He had that washed and combed look of an Outlander.

Old Bascomb stood agape, not taking the proffered hand at first. Sim grinned.

"Now then, Seth," he admonished good-naturedly, "don't tell me you'd ever forget a born Yaater!"

"Well boom me out," barked Romeo, "if it ain't Sim Yarboro, growed up!"

Seth grinned until his upper choppers began to loosen. He shoved them back up with his thumb and grabbed Sim's hand and pumped it like he had a well full of mountain liquor. Then everyone rushed in and made a welcome home brotherhood out of it. Even the older women snapped their dresstails in the excitement. And you could see the younger ones itching shamelessly, with ready sin in their eyes. Naturally, the womenfolk were mighty intrigued over Sim's limp, figuring it was his war injury, but he laughed and said it was just a bruised knee from football practice.

But he did look robust and handsome, and all the girls agreed when Romeo said, "I do fancy a feller with the world by the tail on a downhill pull, and is atwistin' it to his liken'."

Someplace along the line one of the women got in about his mother's death and what a fine funeral it had been, and right then a lot of the fun went out of Sim. For the first time there was a dark, angry look that was enough of Junius to brand Sim for a Yarboro.

"You never let us know," Seth said kinda gently. "The Reverend Mr. Grocer would have held it over 'til you got here."

Sim nodded briefly; it was understandable. He cast his eye over the mail day assembly. None of his kinfolk was present.

"Any special reason the Yarboro clan isn't represented at mail time?"

"Bub and Pete is fixtures at the P&X Mills. They don't never git in," Seth explained. "And your sisters Marthy and Pebby is both aflirtin' with a midwife. You know Marthy married the Jenkin's kid and Pebby's got her clutches on the middle Miller kid."

"Pebby's having a child?" Sim was taken aback. "Why she's not grown up yet!"

Seth shrugged, "She's past thirteen, and like your father said, 'when they're big enough, they're old enough.'"

Sim's face went blank and Romeo chortled.

"Last time I seen the two of them they was both aloomin' up like a backhouse in a high fog." The women bridled and the girls in the background tittered.

Mrs. Jim Perkins said her mind. "You ain't fit to feed with the hawgs, Romeo McFeddor," she spat out, "atalkin' thataway in front of a lot of blameless girls. And you ain't much better, Seth Bascomb." The women turned en masse and flounced away. "You aimin' to stay, son?" said Seth.

"Not exactly." Sim looked over to where Zack Taylor was distributing mail sacks, groceries and drygoods purchases he'd made in the county seat as an accommodation to the housewives. "In truth, I'm paying Zack extra to wait overnight and drive me back in the morning."

Romeo looked scandalized. "That'll hardly give you time to go out and see the old stump ranch or your pa, let alone brush shoulders with the rest of your kinfolk."

"Anybody living at the home place with the old man?"

Seth joined in. "Pebby and her husband. She married the middle Miller cub from Upper Forks. They come in the day your ma died, last Monday, that was. I reckon them kids bin eatin' pretty low on the hawg, him bein' both bogue and satchel-crazy and only just past sixteen, and Pebby bein' too full of seed to move out of her own shadder. Anyway, I hear tell Junius has set 'em up in the cave under the cook room." Sim nodded.

Romeo had been watching. "You ain't interested in how your pa is?" he questioned finally.

Sim hesitated, then as though the words were dragged out of him, asked, "Yes; how is he?"

Romeo nodded approvingly.

"Fine! Strong as ever! Howsomever, he don't lose his temper anymore, like he used to."

"That so?" Sim said tightly.

"Yep, simmered down quite a lot."

"But he's still hale and hearty and in good strength?"

Seth had caught something in Sim's tone and eyed him questioningly. "Well," he said, "after all, he's younger'n Romeo here, and you know what an everlastin' young feller he is."

"Don't forgit he begat the makin's of a baby this last year," Romeo pointed out.

Seth gave his glib fellow Yaater a dirty look. Sim's face had gone first pale and then thunder-dark.

"Yes," his mouth twisted, "I won't forget that."

"If your Ma hadn't been so set on havin' that old midwife she always had for the rest of you chaps," Seth said worriedly, "it might of come right. The way I hear it, that old Ridge woman mommixed it up good."

"Maybe she wanted it mommixed up," Sim said between his teeth. "Maybe she was glad to get shet of the world, Yaates Valley and Junius Yarboro once and for all." As his voice began to rise, he broke with the two men and turned on his heel and crossed blindly through the mail day crowd, who suddenly had lost interest in cutting their weeds, and were standing with craned necks and ears up.

Worm in the Core

Sim walked through the picnic grounds as the young girls flounced, posed and fluttered, shrieking and chitter-chattering, but suddenly becoming doe-eyed and breathlessly still with his passing; then past the horseshoe pits where the young men and boys were, and out onto the Forest Service road. Up the Valley a couple of hundred yards and across the road was the entrance to the Yaates burying ground. Sim made as though to enter, then swerved and went on by.

Without grasping exactly what was taking place, McFeddor had an unconscionable sense of the years slipping back; of Sim never having left the Valley; of the old hateful Junius back again, fisting the boy, Sim. Romeo looked at Seth uneasily and said, "Junius shouldn't ever of ought to have peeled Sim the way he done. Sim's growed up to a bull goose in his own right, but he ain't forgot."

"He's in full seed," Seth admitted. "All six foot, two hundred pounds of him."

"Polished!"

"Seems so!" Doubtfully.

"Polished," Romeo repeated, "like a new-picked pippin, rubbed up and down your shirt bosom—gloss, glow and gleam."

148

"With a worm in the core." Seth looked anxiously out toward the road.

So Seth felt it too!

"Maybe it'd been healthier, he hadn't come home," Romeo fidgeted.

"Would seem a man who'd had six, eight years buckin' circumstances, fightin' enemies in foreign places and gettin' eddicated 'ud lost interest in his shirttail days."

Seth and Romeo had retreated to the steps of the Federal Building. The other citizens pretending anxious interest in their gleaning from the mail truck, were piqued with curiosity and, in a few cases, as concerned as the two on the porch. Some of the women attempted to query Zack Taylor.

What had Sim said on the ride in?

Precious little!

Was he glad to be coming home?

Zack didn't know.

Did he talk about his family?

No, he didn't, and that's a fact.

Was he in good spirits or glum?

Zack shrugged, "Friendly, interested. He laughed some; he just set, mostly."

"Somebody should ought to go up to the Yaraboro place and tell the family Sim is home," one of the women thought.

Her husband said, "No! Keep out of other folks' affairs for once in your life, for Christ sake," and stalked off. She was mighty offended, with tears in her eyes, and got considerable comforting and consolation from the other women.

As Sim had passed through them and out into the road, the girls in the picnic grove were as flitter-minded as pullets with their first rooster. Each one was dreaming of her own variation of the same fantasy theme—to be selected and carried off by Sim Yarboro on his own terms and in a manner she would be unable to resist physically or emotionally and, of course, in a fashion for which she was not accountable.

Each was a-tremble, as though already set aside for Sim's edification and the inevitable submission. The nearness of this powerful hunk of maleness—Eros incarnate—had constricted hearts and muted voices, but as he moved beyond, overwrought nerve centers dammed and tortured by carnal anticipations erupted in shrill, scintillating showers of vociferication. Each, having mentally committed herself as a willing chippy within the full width of her imagination, had for the moment become a miniature hussy, full of dissembling evasions, duplicity and humbug hypocrisy, as a shield against invasion of her prurient desires. A turbulent rage of irrational twitter and chirp fractured the air and arose to the Goddess Nymphomania, until the hysterical flutter resembled a convention of jays and sparrows.

Sim's passage near the young men was pointedly ignored. There had been no pause in their horseshoe games. True, to an observing eye, there was an underlying self-consciousness of jealous discontent against the return of the prodigal. When he turned into the road there burst forth a rumbling undertone of disparagement which came forth in spates of ironic ribaldry to the accompaniment of snickers and mocking laughter. It is an interesting but common fact, how the jibe, the sneer, and the scurrilous quip jointly conspired in a group will salve individual uneasiness, even renew a man's self-approval and return to him a facade of confidence.

So it was that Sim Yarboro's homecoming reception was cloaked in a shimmering haze of emotional vibrations as varied as they were violent. None of which, it should be stated, penetrated his awareness; and none of which, had he been aware, would have pierced his epidermis; that casing already being packed to bursting with the young man's own unexpected tensions.

He had walked perhaps fifty yards beyond the graveyard entrance and then, on impulse, had swerved from the road into the Lodgepole thicket. After a few steps he sat down on an outcropping of rock, hidden by a curtain of greenery from the road.

Until his arrival, he had forgotten what the Yaate Country was. His return had been dictated by an undeniable urge. His mother's death had summoned him and he had responded, unconscious of any subtle implications. Now, the impact of childhood memories bore down on him with frightening weight. He had long considered the Yaate merely as an unpleasant place to reside; he had remembered his mother as a patient, ineffectual force against the tyranny of his father; he had come to think of his father, not with the live coal of burning hatred in the pit of his stomach, but rather as a disagreeable, heavy-handed man, now out of his life.

But here it was back again. The yearning love he had held for his mother; the love she had returned; the memories of the times she had crept to his bed in the night and held him in her arms and cried with him over bruised flesh and bruised spirit—the evidence of his father's unrelenting harshness. She had loved him more than she had loved her husband. At least it had seemed so in those moments of helpless, hopeless yearning.

For the first time now, he wondered whether his leaving may not have been the final crushing blow for her. Sim brooded over the new thought. She had loved him and he had deserted her. Perhaps if he had not gone, she might not have let his father force this sixth and fatal pregnancy upon her. Perhaps she had sought consolation in a new child to take his, Sim's, place. Sim remembered his brothers and sisters as small unlovable creatures; trifling images of his father. He could not conceive of them as being a consolation to her.

Sim stirred in confusion, made up basically of anger. So his father once more had taken advantage of her loneliness and had, at last, killed her. That much was clear! Whatever his own shortcomings, and he saw these imperfectly and confessed them, still her death was his father's doing.

The more Sim dwelled upon the thought, the more he trembled with all the old childhood fear and rage against Junius Yarboro. By now he was overwhelmed with a nostalgia that permeated every breath of the Yaates Valley air he drew in; he was filled with his old, old childhood loneliness for his mother. Gripping his fists into tight knots, he there and then rededicated a vengeful heart against his father.

He rose to his feet and was moving back onto the road before he realized he was being impelled to search out his mother's grave.

Three Mistresses

It may be pertinent at this time to suggest some of the events pertaining to Sim's several years among the Out-landers, which vary somewhat, in degree if not in fact, with his conscious meditations from which he is at the moment walking away.

Sim had had three mistresses of some duration, each of whom was of an age to have begotten him; specifically, somewhat of the age of his own mother. The first had been his landlady while he worked in the Redwood timber along the northern coast of California. She had made him com-fortable beyond her bed, had fed him at her own table, washed and mended, and as often as not had tucked him in, kissed him and shut the door softly behind her. She often said it was a comfort to have a man about the house and, inasmuch as the whole community called her "Ma"—Ma Jeffery's Rooming House—it pleased Sim to call her Ma, and he very often felt she was.

His second affair of a sustained duration was with an English woman while his paratroop outfit was stationed for six months in the Near East. There were a wide variety of opportunities among girls of every race imaginable and of his own age. The paratroopers' reputation as the cream of America's rugged young manhood had preceded his arrival, and the uniforms and paraphernalia sustained the promise to melt many tender young hearts. However, Sim met a Mrs. Maude Forsythe, a widow whose only son, a year older than

Sim, had been killed with the British Colonial troops in
Africa.

Mrs. Forsythe had lent herself as a volunteer government
worker, and had at every opportunity invited American and
British boys to her quarters. When it had been Sim's good
fortune, he had found the answer to a dull, persisting ache;
and evidently so had Mrs. Forsythe. An arrangement, easily
entered into and satisfying to both, developed and maintained itself until the gray day Sim was flown a thousand
miles and dropped on a battlefield.

His third mother-son attachment still is in effect. Florence Cartwright had divorced her husband fifteen years
before, on the grounds of incompatibility. He was a professor
of Advanced Psychology at the University of California; a
self-sufficient, stubborn man who had no inclination to
clutter up his house nor his life with children.

Florence, a full professor of Modern Languages, would
have foregone her career in education for the role of mother.
Now at forty-seven, marriage, in her mind, was out of the
question. After the divorce, she had retained the same
house on Cypress Road behind the Berkeley campus. When
the population exploded and the sudden emphasis on college
education flooded the university, a desperate student housing
shortage ensued. Mrs. Cartwright was prevailed upon, against
her better judgment, to open a spare bedroom. Her extreme
reluctance caused her to insist on her right to pick and
choose her candidate.

When Sim was sent to her from the San Francisco
Presidio Military Hospital, he was still a partial convalescent.
He had nearly lost both feet from gangrene as a result of ten
wicked days, sunk to his ankles and fighting for his life in a
stinking field of mud and water, reeking with the stench of
human excrescence and further befouled by the decaying
carcasses of bloated dogs and native soldiers. The magic of
modern medicine and the magnificence of his own physique

stood him in good stead. Both feet were healthy again, but still-tender flesh and lack of exercise had brought Sim to Florence Cartwright's door on crutches.

Whether the crutches, the hospital pallor, or an admission to being a product of a fantastic, never-before-heard-of place called Yaates Valley, Montana, was the basis of Florence's initial attraction, can only be surmised, but the true underlying stimuli were a reasonable facsimile of his two earlier experiences.

He had once again found his mother; she the child so long denied her.

This is not a record of how, when, or why the relationship, in due course, changed from compatible strangers to something more intimate and mutually satisfying; only of the fact that it did occur.

But this was only the love pattern. Simultaneously and just as unconsciously, Sim relived again and again a passionate and violent hate pattern—a fierce anger against a ruthless paternal parent, which turned every man of authority, every boss, every overseer, into a father figure.

It was this repetitive hate theme which accounts for those early reports of Sim's drifting migration, which came back to us while still within range of Yaates Valley's human radar screen. In the Washington wheatfields he had laid down his pitchfork and walked off when an irate foreman gave his binder-crew the devil for falling behind schedule.

In the Crater Lake National Park he went after a sarcastic uniformed pipsqueak of a Forest Service official with a stick of firewood which bystanders wrestled from him, and was summarily dismissed.

He held to his Redwood lumber camp job for eight months—the steadying influence of "Ma"—but here too, came a time when he struck a timber boss with the flat of a shovel. He kept out of jail by the simple process of vanishing from camp.

The Army caught up with him in San Francisco, and gave him his closest call with disaster. Originally, he had been with the infantry, but when a sadistic sergeant at Camp Pendleton ripped him to the raw for a full half-hour's hiding, Sim suddenly lunged out and smashed his nose, opening a gusher of blood, military court-martial was inevitable.

Two circumstances saved Sim. The Commandant had furious and personal aversion to malicious cruelty in any form. The tactics of this particular sergeant had been called to his attention before. When he saw Sim for himself, it went against his gorge to send such a fine specimen of potential fighting man into confinement.

The call was out for volunteers in paratroop training and, after grave consideration, Sim was offered his choice: face prison or volunteer for paratroop training. Sim volunteered.

Nothing could have suited Sim better in this world of gruelling discipline. The paratroopers were an outfit in which officers and men shared equal jeopardy, were expendable to the same degree, and mutually shared mental and physical strain. Actually, the added responsibility of the officers gave the men an edge. Such group morale, comradery and fellow feeling, between men and men, and men and officers, as grew out of equal hardship, dangers and discipline, Sim had never known before, and the experience was a pure joy to a lacerated spirit. It was at once the ruggedest, and the happiest, time of his misfit life.

By the second year at the university, Sim's feet were fit and his health was such that he yearned for physical activity. He was attracted to the football field and by midseason had found a place on the second string squad. But now the old pattern was working again. Two weeks before the California-Stanford game, he had an argument with the line coach. One week before the game, in final signal practice and skirmishes against the first squad, this same coach yanked him out of the line—that is, physically yanked him from behind, as he crouched for a play, so that he sat back violently on his bottom. In his rage, without rising, he tackled the coach and was on top of him—once again an unthinking paratrooper with an enemy beneath him. He was yanked off before any great damage was done, but that was the end of his football career.

Junius Yarboro

None of this was in Sim's mind as he walked back down the road to the graveyard. He simply wished to say goodbye to his mother and catch the mail truck back to the county seat with Zack Taylor.

He came on the grave unexpectedly. The new earth, the raw mound, the inferior concrete markers at head and foot—all were cruelly cold and unfinished, so unlike the neat grass-grown grave he had envisioned. It was a brutal slap in the face; as though the noon whistle had blown and the artisans had dropped their tools.

Again he tasted the bitter bile of unreasoning anger against his father. He had killed her and, still not satisfied, added this ignominy of careless indifference. Reason could have told him it took time to grow grass and flowers; that a stone cutter in Kalispell or Sand Point even now might be cutting a proper headstone. Reason might have told him, but he was listening only to ragged, raging emotions.

He sank down on a yew stump, brooding. A grave among the stumps. He always had known the Yaates Cemetery was full of stumps, just as so many Montana and Idaho farms still were stump land. It had not occurred to him before, but now he saw everything in this blighted valley as raw, ugly, neglected and somehow indecent.

A shadow fell upon him. He glanced up. A ragged native, somewhat fifty or sixtyish, with watery pale blue eyes and a droopy, neglected mustache, stood silently eyeing him. Sim's first reaction was outrage at any intrusion on his private sorrow. His store of mute resentment lasted a long thirty seconds before realization seeped in.

He was looking upon his father!

He was looking upon Junius Yarboro.

And he was looking upon a man wholly at a loss.

"Where's my son, Sim?" There was bewilderment in the pale eyes and in the voice. "They said he'd come home."

Sim rose unsteadily.

"I'm Sim," he said, hardly conscious of the grim response. For the instant he was totally unaware of his intentions, now that he was face-to-face with the man who had haunted his life for as long as he could remember.

Disbelief struggled with a striving for recognition in the older man's face.

Abruptly, without premeditation, Sim grasped Junius by the wrist, yanked him close, sat back on the stump, hauling Junius face down across his knees and began to wallop him with his open hand. Once begun, he couldn't stop. It went on and on until his arm ached and his hand felt swollen and broken.

Junius, after a first heartless effort at escape, had lay unresisting, as grotesquely inert as a heap of old sougans. He had no heart, no will, to resist. A man who had fought Montana summers and winters and struggled to maintain himself and a big family on the thin-soiled stump land of the Yaates, was as sound and rugged and invincible at sixty as an ordinary man at twenty-five. So it was not a lack of strength. Although, in a knock-down fight, the younger man probably would have survived on sheer stamina.

It was finished as abruptly as it began. Sim stood up, hauling his father to his feet.

"Does that remind you of anything?" he demanded, hoarse with passion.

There were tears of shame, humiliation, defeat, on Junius' face. Not anger, not surprise, not even misunderstanding.

Junius took a deep shaken breath, hesitated, wavered, then slowly turned and wandered off, going in no particular direction for no particular reason.

Sim slumped down on the stump, buried his face in his hands, and wept.

A shadowy figure tiptoed away among the trees. It was Romeo McFeddor.

"Cripes," he said in an awed whisper. "Cripes in the high corn!"

PART VII

Ella Corvell's Girl

August, 1940

The day before Granny Culbertson's son Marvin returned to Yaates Valley from three years of Missoula Medical School was the August afternoon we buried Ella Corvell's girl, Eve. It was a sorry time. Even the Rev. Mr. Grocer had tears in his eyes, and the way the women sat and mourned in their handkerchiefs would have made an Outlander wonder.

The circumstances of this bad business are so painful they hardly bear telling. It was partly that Eve had just passed her sixteenth birthday; so pretty, young, and already said to be promised to Hal Morgan's boy, Wayne. The whole valley had enjoyed this lacy-valentine kind of romance. Eve so pert and joyful and Wayne kinda' handsome and earnest in a dark mysterious sort of way made folks look forward to them belonging to each other.

That alone made death seem a personal tragedy to all of us, but now murder had turned it into a city slum-basement crime! Murder out of lust and perversion should be a product of propinquity; of swarming beehives of humanity. Folks just weren't prepared for sex and violence out under miles of sky where a man has to walk or ride for hours sometimes just to brush shoulders with another human being. To make it even worse, Yaaters had no experience or conception of the caliber of man nor type of mind that could be this secret and foul.

Montana men, women and even children just naturally understand the robust appetites of nature. Every man is expected to get his share and every woman naturally contributes at the proper time, place and circumstance. With this broad working plan and ready access, there is no more excuse to murder from lustful motives than for a man to crush a bed of Johnny-jump-ups when he might just as easily step around them.

These were some of the elements which contributed to the morbid drama of Eve's last rites, along with the unnerving realization that the matter wasn't ending here. The mystery of who and why was still to haunt us. Add to this the knowledge that it was not possible for an Outlander to enter Yaates Valley without it immediately becoming known and spreading like a crown fire in a hot July wind. A newcomer was known everywhere: The Forks, Shadow Creek, Adobe Flat, Bates Ranch, Salt Creek, Jefferies' Fish Hatchery, Crawford's Mine, the P&X Lumber Mill, Mt. Baldy Camp No. Three, the Upper Forks!

Government agents had encountered this phenomenon over and over; the Forest Service, the Revenue Men, Game Wardens, the Sheriff; even the weekly rural mail truck. It was the womenfolk, of course.

There had been no Outlander for over a week before Eve was strangled with her own petticoat and left in a Lodgepole thicket, a hundred yards off the main Forest Service road. So the killer was a Yaater; one of ourselves, almost certainly among us here at the graveside.

Romeo McFeddor remarked that he wouldn't be surprised that half of the gnashing of teeth was for Eve and the other half just plain terror of every woman, fearful lest her own husband had done it. Seth Bascomb, elder statesman for Yaates Valley, looked sharply at Romeo and said talk like that could point the finger of suspicion mighty close to home. After that Romeo shut up.

Not only was it frightening to be rubbing elbows with an unidentified murderer, but exasperating not to be able to unburden oneself for fear the ear we were bending might as likely as not belong to the principal subject of conversation.

The final straw for the distraught mourners was the last-minute word that the casket was not to be opened. The Rev. Grocer had viewed the remains earlier and pronounced the deceased in no fit state to confront the public gaze. It was well the pallbearers had begun to lower the casket; otherwise a swarm of militant women would have overwhelmed them and torn off the lid. As it was, there was little to do but stand about in indignation and fresh tears and abuse the Rev. Grocer.

This was little or no burden to the Reverend as Yaates Valley was but one of five communities dividing his professional attention. He was not a Yaates man and came every third Sunday for divine services, and on special wedding or funeral calls.

Two days after Eve's funeral and Marvin's arrival home, his parcels came from Missoula on the weekly mail truck and were dumped off on the porch of the Federal Building, same being Seth Bascomb's cabin. Besides the battered imitation leather suitcase, a suitbox tied with hemp cord, and a cardboard beer carton bulging with books, there was a heavier reinforced wooden box, which had a queer unpleasant smell. Anyone familiar with the City Morgue, or the dissecting laboratory of a medical school, would have identified the smell at once.

Romeo was relaxing on the steps making little sticks

out of big sticks with his "skinning knife" when the mail truck drew up and Zack Taylor climbed down to drop off Marvin's effects. He was early this week, and Romeo was the only citizen in sight. The box took considerable moving, but Romeo made no effort to assist, whereupon Zack swore and dropped it on the porch as near Romeo's fingers as he dared and let it sit. Romeo got his first whiff.

"Good God," he exclaimed, "Marvin's settin' up a glue factory, and the whole shebang's got putrid on its way in."

"Smells to me like a *hide* factory," Zack commented, meaning a tannery. "Marvin must not gonna be a very high-class doctor; man'd have to be in considerable pain to go to a doctor this far gone."

"You gotta get the hang of doctorin'," explained Romeo tolerantly. "Medicine's like skinnin' a bear or castratin' a cat." He looked at the long blade of his hunting knife with affection. "You ruin a few hides and turn out some awful sick kitties before you get the knack."

"Ain't no sich kitty in *that* box," Zack asserted, eyeing the offending container. "Could be a decomposed bear hide, maybe."

Romeo moved over to the other end of the steps, away from the box.

"Don't guess medical students do much bear skinning behind them secret college doors."

Zack stared. "What *do* they skin?"

"Folks!"

Zack looked at the big box with undisguised prejudice.

"Well, they don't actually *skin* 'em," Romeo amended.

"At least I don't *know* if they skin 'em. It's called dissection!"

Zack got in the mail truck, backed around and headed out of the valley. This was not like Zack. On ordinary mail days he waited for the population. Almost every family would be represented before the morning was over; already assembling down in the picnic area were two rusty sedans, a dilapidated jeep, a vintage dump truck and four cattle ponies.

This Friday promised to be better attended than ordinary; people were still under the influence of Wednesday's funeral and there was need to test community temper against their individual qualms.

Uppermost and foremost was the haunting knowledge of the criminal in their midst. But all that mail day no one could come right out about it! How fearful the innocent can feel. Fear of saying too much or too little; fear of drawing unfortunate attention to ourselves! And withal a queer shamefaced "mass guilt." A community sense that "as one among us is guilty, so are we all tainted."

The crime, the criminal, the criminal's victim, Eve's burial, and Marvin's putrid box shared largely in the limelight with the distribution of the weekly mail accumulation, the groceries, and equipment Zack had brought. His early departure caused considerable dissatisfaction.

A few women owed him for their deliveries; others had shopping lists of necessities they'd been depending on Zack to bring next mail day. The result was an unusual amount of grumbling, touchiness and explosiveness. Despite the gorge of events for gossip, nobody felt in the mood for sociability. Some who'd brought picnic lunches, expecting to make a day of it, ate early and packed up for home. The rest picked up their mail sacks, stood around for a few minutes, felt the unwholesomeness in the atmosphere and cleared out. It was even more disappointing and frustrating than Wednesday's funeral.

By three o'clock everyone was gone except Romeo and Seth. At a quarter after, Seth excused himself with a mail-order catalogue and disappeared around back of the Federal Building.

Marvin didn't arrive down from Granny's Salt Creek cabin, a long rutty seven miles, until close on to three-thirty. He was pushing a good-sized wheelbarrow. Romeo brightened and put up his whittling at the sight of Marvin, but his tailbone remained glued to the top step.

"Afternoon, Marvin," he welcomed. "Your stuff's up here on the porch."

Marvin nodded and began putting the oversized packing case in the bed of the barrow.

"You aim to wheel that load all the way up Salt Crik by yourself?"

"Unless you want to come along and help!" Marvin invited.

"No, no," said Romeo hastily. "Don't depend on me."

"Proud for your company," Marvin urged, tying the box securely and piling on the cardboard boxes and the suitcase. "You could catch me up on the gossip."

"Don't need me to carry boxes," Romeo said grumpy. "Besides, doctors don't want me pushin' no wheelbarrows."

"Oh? What doctors?"

"All of them," Romeo rubbed his chest authoritatively. "I'm a heart case."

Marvin grinned. "Well, would it be bad for you to walk along beside me while I pushed the wheelbarrow?"

Romeo arose with alacrity. "That," he said, "is allowable. Furthermore, you want me to, when we get to Joe Lancer's I'll get him to let you borrow one of his pack mules."

"I might just do that," Marvin agreed. "Just a minute," he said, and went inside to pick up the mail bag and a box of dry groceries which Granny Culbertson had ordered last mail day. Marvin hadn't seen Seth yet, so he yelled, "Hello," hoping Bascomb was around.

Seth yelled from out back that he was on The Throne and Marvin had caught him with his pants down, and he'd be out in half-an-hour.

Marvin yelled back he couldn't wait.

Old Seth said he was sorry, but at his time of life a half-hour was par for the course so he'd see Marvin next time he was down.

Marvin joined Romeo out front, put his mail sack and groceries on top of the barrow, remarking if old Bascomb was *that* constipated he maybe needed medical advice.

He took a good grip on the barrow handles and headed up the Forest Service road.

Romeo sauntered beside him.

"Only place Seth's constipated is in his sense of what's fit and natural," he said. "Seth don't need no doctor; what *he* needs is a *woman*."

Marvin looked disbelieving!

Romeo just grinned and shrugged. "How's Granny?" he asked.

"Mother doesn't change much; just old and set in her

ways." Marvin was indifferently affectionate. "Forgot most of the past and present; full of hellfire and brimstone predictions for the future." To the rest of the valley Granny Culbertson was a filthy witch-like character; hadn't been clear in mind nor clean in body in fifty years—fifty-two to be exact! That was when her husband, Fred Culbertson, went to Alaska with a prostitute from a dance hall down at the county seat. The word came back that both Fred and the girl made their fortunes, went on to live handsomely in San Francisco and New York, and the next anyone knew they'd gone down on the *Lusitania*. Granny never even tried to find out whether she'd been legally divorced. There had been a lot of valley gossip about her inheritance, but nothing ever came of it.

Marvin actually was not flesh of Granny's flesh nor blood of her blood. At least no one thought so, and neither Granny nor Marvin ever said. First anyone knew about Marvin was the day twenty-two or -three years ago when Seth Bascomb rode up Salt Creek to bring Granny her mail. She hadn't been down to the Federal Building for three weeks.

When things like that happened, Seth, feeling obligated as the eldest citizen, always made it a point to investigate. Well, the reason for Granny's disinterest in mail day was apparent at once. Granny was seated on her front stoop, a mangy dog at her feet; an old sow on the porch between her and the door stretched comfortably on her side nursing a litter of eleven. Chickens lined the porch rail, picking lice from their feathers; and in Granny's arms, being lovingly fed from a medicine bottle and a sugar tit, was a two-month-old baby boy.

Nobody knows to this day where Marvin come from, save that obviously he was not out of Granny's withered old womb. There was considerable talk that he was one of the by-products of Fred Culbertson's misspent life, but nothing came out after his death. But from the day of his arrival, he was dearly loved and tenderly cared for by the dirty irresponsible old woman, and it was obvious from the beginning he was superior.

He taught himself to read and in adolescence decided on medicine for a career. Granny's Salt Creek cabin was isolated and Granny's own fey ways were not conducive to neighborliness, so that Marvin grew up isolated and out of the way, but definitely integrated as part and parcel of Yaates Valley community life and lore. We all had considerable admiration for his erudite tendencies, but little understanding of his aims or ambitions.

"What you aimin' to do, now you're back, son?" Romeo asked, ambling along casually beside the barrow.

"Get my old job back timekeeping at the mill; I expect they can still use a man."

"Man with a pencil," agreed Romeo. "Not many folks up here good with a pencil. What about *that stuff?*" he nodded at Marvin's cargo.

Marvin grinned, "You know that big root cellar; the one Granny gave up using before I came to roost on her doorstep?"

Romeo remembered.

"Well, I cleaned it out yesterday; ran an air vent and a stove pipe down through the sod roof; built some benches, tables, and installed that old rusty Franklin stove that's been out in the shed under the hay since I can remember."

"Settin' up housekeeping separate from Granny?" Romeo was real surprised.

"My own private laboratory." Satisfaction was in Marvin's voice. "Oh nothing but bare essentials; dissecting table I built myself; cut the top out of a fifty-gallon drum for a formaldehyde tank; I've got my dissection kit, retorts, microscopes, two good Coleman lamps and some jars of solution and specimens."

If Marvin had been looking at Romeo's face he might have ended his confidence then and there. But he was indulging himself, the road was rutty, the wheelbarrow heavy, so he was rattling on.

"I ran out of money at Missoula, but I didn't run out of brains, so while I'm earning something for next year at school, I'll work nights on my books and what I can't find out from the printed page, I'll dig into with my scalpel. Any volunteers for a cadaver?" He set down the barrow, wiped his face which was as red and sweaty as it was cheerful. Unfortunately, he took this opportunity to change the subject.

"Granny tells me little Eve Corvell was buried yesterday?" he said with an inquiring, sympathetic look. Romeo's eyes opened with a sort of fascinated horror.

Marvin missed the implication. "Well, she was, wasn't she? I never can be sure whether Granny's ramblings are actual-factual or moonbeams and cobwebs."

"She was for a fact," Romeo agreed uneasily.

"Murdered?"

Romeo nodded again.

"Strangled and raped, Granny says?"

Romeo acquiesced.

"Murderer still at large?"

Romeo continued mute but nodded.

"No one under suspicion?"

A shake of the head.

"One of our own Yaaters according to Granny." Marvin stood up. "Too bad," he said, hunching over the barrow handles and heaving against the load.

Romeo lagged as though he had sufficient cud to chew on and contemplated breaking away; then deciding against it, caught up. He walked along beside Marvin for almost a quarter of a mile before he spoke.

"With all them females over on the Ridge big enough, willing enough, and in most cases purty enough, why'd a man want to go out of his way to do what he done to Eve?" he wondered morosely. "She was harmless; she wasn't flirty; she was about the happiest thing in the valley; and she was the only thing the whole community had common pride in. So why'd somebody strangle her for what he could get *give* to him behind 'most any bush?"

Marvin shrugged, "Perverseness."

"What?"

"To want what you can't have; to reject what comes easily and costs nothing."

"Honest to Christ," muttered Romeo, recognizing both the truth and hopelessness.

Marvin shifted ground again. "You were talking about the Ridge. The women over there really pretty?"

"Some of them," Romeo grinned. "All *my* daughters are."

"Your daughters?"

Romeo nodded with a sort of rakish, sheepish grin. "I must have fifteen, twenty orphan kids over on the Ridge. I made a terrible mistake with one of them. . . . I didn't realize how big some of 'em's getting to be. Couple of winters ago, I sent over for somebody to keep me warm durin' the cold weather; specially durin' the snowed-in season, and a right pretty young woman come to the cabin. And you want to know, I come darn near spendin' the whole winter in sin with my own daughter. She never *did* know, but I got a sneaky feelin' she was too much like me, and I checked up; sure enough, she was one of the first kids I'd farmed out over yonder on the Ridge seventeen, eighteen year before."

"What'd you do, send her back?" You could believe only about half of anything Romeo told you, and you never knew which half was the truth; but he made amusing listening.

"No, that was the winter Joe Lancer brought in a middle-aged woman from over in Kalispell. She was a little too buxom for what Joe had in mind, so's I made a deal with him. . . . I'd take Mrs. Purdy, a hundred and sixty-eight pounds barefooted and shiftless, a pack saddle I'd had my eye on, and give him Lily Mae."

"Lily Mae was your daughter?"

"But nobody knowed that. In the spring Mrs. Purdy went back to Kalispell where she had a job waitin' on tables in the hotel, and Lily Mae went back up on the Ridge."

"She didn't want to stay?"

"Nope. Us Yaaters is too civilized for folks raised Ridge style. You know, Marvin," Romeo said out of sudden thought, "you're the first and only child I ever know of, born a bastard and left on a Yaater's doorstep. You ever stop to think of that?"

Marvin put down the barrow again, sat on one handle

and took out his handkerchief. "You think that's important?" he asked.

"Well, look at it for yourself. Last spring I made out seven pregnancies here in the valley that didn't have no brand on 'em. You know and I know that every mother's daughter of them seven girls had a baby; ain't no abortion business up in *these hills* by God! But where *is* the babies today?"

Marvin nodded. "The Ridge," he agreed. "And that's something I want to do something about, once I'm a doctor."

"You ain't plannin' to start no abortion mill?" Romeo said with dismay.

"No, but neither do I like the idea of the Ridge continuing as a combined orphanage and baby farm for unwanted Yaates Valley children. Poor little bastards."

"Sure, sure, but what I was getting around to," said Romeo not interested in the social welfare problem, "was why wasn't *you* sent to the Ridge?"

Marvin stared. "I've never thought about it," he muttered.

Romeo nodded, "Other folks have. All other illegits vanish up on the Ridge. . . . How come, not *you*?"

"Maybe I wasn't illegitimate."

"Then why was you left on a doorstep?"

"I don't know; especially, why was I left on Granny Culbertson's step?"

"This the first time you ever talked to any Yaater about yourself?"

Marvin nodded.

"Well, us Yaaters figured maybe you was the son of Fred Culbertson and some day would get a pile of dough from the estate him and that whore he run off with, mined out of the Klondikers up in Alaska."

Marvin shook his head. "I don't think so." He got up, spit on his hands and grabbed the handlebars again. Romeo followed.

"Naturally, you was left on Granny's step on account she was old, lonesome, and somebody knew she'd hunger after a baby and would yearn over you; they also know'd if you was to be left on any other Yaater's doorstep, you'd be sent off up the Ridge quicker'n bunny love."

When they got to Joe Lancer's place Romeo was as good as his word about getting pack mules. He even deigned to help cinch on the pack saddles and lash on the cargo.

"I Came Prepared"

The Spider Creek Forks was a mile or more from the Corvell cabin and where Jennie Loughner's washed-out dirt road branched off from the graveled main Forest Service road to wander a rugged up and down nine miles along Spider Creek to end at Jennie's. It had been a convenient rendezvous for Eve, a safe place to get home from alone after dark, and had the added advantage of seclusion.

A heavy Lodgepole pine thicket began here which extended to and beyond the Canadian Border to the north and over into Idaho and the primitive area to the east. A frightening place to be lost in, for a thicket is not only made up of thirty- and forty-foot mature trees but saplings as thickly sown by the hand of God as any man-made wheat field, relieved only in occasional spots by rock projections or barren soil.

Wayne had been waiting since eight o'clock in no graceful frame of mind when Eve finally arrived. He might be a man in love, but he was an ungracious one.

"I never heard of such damned nonsense," he greeted. "Why couldn't I have come to your house? It's almost ten."

Even so, the last glimmering light of day still lingered in the sky reluctant to leave this northern beauty.

"I had to wait until my mother was asleep."

175

Eve slipped from the road, in among the interlacing trees, to be greeted by a frantic snuffling, scampering and scurrying. A yearling cinnamon cub broke cover and legged it up the Spider Creek road like a cur dog with a tin can tied to his tail.

Wayne, who was at Eve's heels, swore, but after the first jarring start Eve laughed softly and forgot the bear immediately as she pushed further in among the trees until they were lost to the road.

Without ado she turned, letting her coat fall open, and gave herself ardently to Wayne, her arms about his neck, her mouth moist against his and her young body straining eagerly. After his first instant of incomprehension, he responded as recklessly as she to the communion.

But only momentarily. He recovered as quickly as he'd succumbed and pulled her arms from about his neck roughly.

"What are you, a Ridge woman?" he demanded thickly.

"I came prepared," Eve gloated, "couldn't you tell?"

"You done what?"

"Here, feel under my coat. Just my dress and petticoat."

Wayne stonily rejected the invitation, but his eyes glowed red in the gathering dusk.

"What is this anyway?"

"Why would a boy bother to marry a girl if he could have her anyway?" Eve's voice was warm and inviting.

When Wayne stood thunderstruck, Eve went on, "You ever have a girl? Well, here's your chance." She came a step closer. "The girls all think you're still a virgin. They think it's funny."

An inarticulate protest arose in his throat, but his tongue was paralyzed.

"Louise Ackerman's brother says the boys think you're cut. He told Louise you never been up on the Ridge with the boys!" There was maddening compassion in her voice. "Maybe you're afraid of strange girls, but you don't have to be afraid of me."

Then Eve said what was at the bottom of her mind from the beginning. "I wouldn't make you a good wife, but wouldn't you like to know I'd belonged to you just once? All I want is fifty dollars."

A vast roaring storm descended on Wayne; the sky was full of lightning, the heavens full of thunder, there was the rush of tremendous wind in his ears and the earth rose and fell like the breast of an angry ocean. Wayne knew nothing but the tortured cataclysmic disturbance of an unhinged universe.

"Cutting Up A Body"

It was on the fourth day that Wayne Morgan discovered the desecration. He'd gone alone in the twilight
to say goodnight to Eve as he'd done each evening since
her funeral. A northern Montana August night comes
down thick, heavy, and velvety dark just before midnight.
So it was perhaps nine-thirty or ten o'clock when Wayne
crossed under the entrance grove of cedar and spruce
and entered the violet-tinted clearing. His attention was
distracted by the sudden flushing and swooping of a great
horned owl, so that he was almost at his rendezvous when
his eyes turned earthward and saw the appalling violation.
Shambles himself, cloven-hoof and spiked-tail had been
there in person. The fresh earth of the new-turned grave,
not yet packed, was scattered and marred; the cut flowers
trampled, vases and containers smashed.

The distress and shock of this new outrage was a
community-wide concern. It was obviously the mischief
of a rogue bear, although no one could remember another
such incident.

Neither Seth nor Romeo nor Sam Jones, the valley's
three best hunters and trackers, could find a single
animal track or spoor. Sam Jones confided to Romeo
that it looked more like the work of timber wolves, only
what would timber wolves be doing down so low in
August, and even if they were, why dig for a buried
corpse when God knows the woods were starting with
live game. And why no wolf signs?

Romeo didn't think it was either bear or wolves. And Seth agreed. Personally, Seth suspected some of them teenage brats from Upper Forks making free with girls from the Ridge, and if he could catch 'em romping in the cemetery he'd give them such a load of rock salt in their behinds, they'd *never* sit down again.

Seth said them Upper Fork young ones was getting so's they thought that any plot of grass wide enough for a girl's backside was a legitimate cat house, and By Sooty, any girl who'd forget herself in a graveyard was deserving to face the consequences.

Romeo didn't think it was kids either. First place, Eve's killer was somewhere about. He'd noticed everybody was keeping closer to home; especially girls of the age for a "lark in the park" as the saying goes. Besides, there were no footprints except Wayne's, which were all over the place, naturally so with him visiting the grave as often as he had.

The plot was graded to its former neatness, flowers replaced, and all signs of maliciousness wiped out. Seth saw to that.

It was the very next afternoon that Romeo, walking up the Forest Service road, came across young Hal Morgan, Wayne's adolescent brother, and Hodge Sweeney's boy Bert, the one with the cleft palate. They were a couple of scared kids hightailin' it for home with a message, and it took Romeo exactly ten seconds to get the gist of it.

"Marvin Culbertson is up at Granny's place cutting up a human being."

Romeo's eyes popped. "You're sure?"

The boys were sure. They'd gone up Salt Creek looking to find beaver signs for next winter's trap lines. They'd bypassed Granny's place on the way up, but coming back they'd sneaked in to get a look at the old woman. They didn't see her, but they did see Marvin come out of the big root cellar and go to Granny's cabin. He locked the cellar door. Well, nobody locks a root cellar door in the Yaate, so naturally the boys were curious.

While Bert Sweeney kept a lookout, young Hal sprung the padlock by hitting it sharply with a rock.

"And right there on a table was a naked arm—" A greenish look came over the boy's complexion and he turned his back and began to disgorge himself with a fearful retching. Bert Sweeney looked at his co-conspirator for one long second, then tore off down the road, his own private terrors close on his heels.

Romeo stood patiently by until most of the agony was over, and then handed Hal a bandana to wipe away the scum and sweat.

"Was it a girl's arm?" he asked gently.

The boy gave him one stricken look and began to sob violently. Romeo touched his shoulder sympathetically, but the boy wrenched away and flew after young Sweeney. Once the boy was out of sight there seemed to be considerable indecision in Romeo. He crossed over to the side of the road, sat down on a fragment of a stump, took a goose quill toothpick out of his vest pocket, absently scratched his ear with it and then set to work on his teeth. Maybe an hour later he rose and started a lounging negligent stroll toward Salt Creek.

Wayne Morgan and his father, Hal Senior, were seated on the steps of the Federal Building when Hal

Junior came into view. Father and son were paying heed to Seth on the matter of the desecration and gleaning what comfort they could.

"Wild animals or them Upper Fork kids," Seth was reiterating with the gravity of an old stork oracle. "That's the answer and don't worry no more about it. We've got the grave looking nice again, and I'm close enough here to do a little night watching for a while. If there's any going's on in the cemetery unfit for the community—animal *or* kids, I'll settle it for good and all."

Wayne sat staring at the ground between his knees, his arms folded across his middle as though suffering a gnawing bellyache. Hal Senior looked up gratefully to Seth and that's when he spied young Hal cutting down the road like he'd been sent for.

"What's snapping at Hal's shirttail?" his father muttered. Seeing the men, the boy cut through the picnic parking area and arrived, a little more gray than green now, and a little more spent than when he left Romeo.

"Marvin's cutting up a girl's body," he gasped.

Wayne leaped to his feet. The two older men rose more slowly. Wayne grabbed his brother by the front of his hickory shirt and shook him as though he never intended to stop, until their father separated them. The younger boy sank down on the steps crying.

"What the hell kind of going's on is *that?*" Morgan yelled at his older son.

"Tell him to shut up, then! Tell the kid to shut up!"

"Why?" asked his father finally.

"Tormenting and bedeviling at a time like this;

what's he trying to do, drive me crazy?"

"It's true," stormed Hal. "Ask Bert Sweeney. He saw it, too; in Granny's root cellar. A girl's arm cut off at the shoulder." Wayne advanced on his brother with a taut, wild, haunting look in his eyes. His father grabbed his arm.

"What's he trying to say?" Wayne babbled. "That's why Eve's grave was tore up? That Marvin's got her body up yonder in his root cellar?"

"Wayne...Wayne," gasped Seth in protest, his weather-beaten cheeks suddenly chalky.

"He ain't sayin' no such thing," yelled his father, provoked beyond reason by the intensity of Wayne's emotion.

"Well, I think that's what he's saying, and I think it's true; just to bedevil me!" He yanked away from his father and ran; not a good healthy determined gait, but a streaking frightened run, with a stumbling erratic lurch to it.

"If he's agoin' after Marvin, there's liable to be blood, guts and feathers all over Hell's half acre," worried his father.

"Wayne ain't goin' *after* anybody," Seth said, staring after the vanishing figure. "That boy's going *away* from anybody."

Romeo Sniffs the Truth

Romeo backed out of Granny Culbertson's big root cellar almost before he was in. Marvin had to do a quick back step to get out of his way, and then as Romeo continued on over to the steps of Granny's hut, he pulled the cellar door shut and snapped the lock on it before joining Romeo.

"See all you came to see?" Marvin asked, sitting down beside his visitor.

Romeo nodded. "Where'd you get it?"

"Not where you're thinking!" Marvin grinned at Romeo's evasive stare. "That's a piece of a cadaver assigned to me for dissection at the medical school. By special dispensation, I was permitted to bring it up here to my private laboratory."

"Yaaters ain't agoin' to stomach unburied pieces of the human carcass in Granny's root cellar," Romeo predicted, indicating his own lack of stomach. "Who is the unfortunate critter?"

Marvin shrugged, "Some indigent who sold her body to the medical school for twelve dollars."

"Why she want to do that? She hungry?"

"No, thirsty!"

"Drunk," muttered Romeo sympathetically.

"Awful," agreed Marvin. "All the time!"

"You know her?"

Marvin shook his head. "I just read her medical history compiled by the police and university authorities as required on all cadavers received by the medical school."

"Things like this'll stay in people's minds," Romeo warned. "They'll hold it against you."

"They'll like me well enough when I get my M.D. and ride up and down the valley, winter, summer, day and night, to save their ungrateful hides."

"I don't know if they will or not."

"I don't either," Marvin agreed wryly. "But I like to hope so."

Romeo shifted the conversation. "How do I *know* that girl's arm in yonder is what you say it is?"

"Want to come back and look again?"

"Sit down!"

Marvin shrugged. "A close examination of the hand should tell you whether it belonged to a young girl or a—"

"I already know without looking."

"How?"

"Anybody could see Eve's grave wasn't really *dug*

into; just surface scratching. Seth...Sam...all of us seen that, just as we seen it wasn't no bear with a bun on, nor mischieffy wolves, nor the Upper Fork hellions. And at least I for one seen it wasn't nobody but one person."

Marvin looked at him sharply.

Romeo moved uneasily. "And it don't make no sense!"

"Well, you didn't tell me that much unless you intended to tell me more."

Romeo slid his hand inside his woolen shirt and scratched himself in the short ribs; took out a snoose box; looked at it as though he was mad at it; "Wayne Morgan!" he muttered.

Marvin was shocked:

"Wayne trampled his sweetheart's grave?"

"I said it don't make sense; but there just wasn't nobody nor nothing else there! Plenty of Wayne everywhere."

"Wayne has been at her grave every evening. Naturally his footprints would be there."

"On the grave?"

Marvin stared!

"Up and down the length of the grave? And then the boot marks swept over with a pine bough to hide the imprints? Only they wasn't hid at all...not from me."

"Wayne trampled the length of Eve's grave?"

Romeo nodded. "Over and over, spurning the top dirt with his feet."

"He must be crazy!"

Romeo was noncommittal.

"And Seth and Sam Jones missed it?"

Romeo grinned, "They ain't no trackers; they *say* they are, but they ain't even good amatooers."

Marvin suddenly snapped his fingers!

"You're right," he exclaimed. "Of course it's Wayne!"

"Well, we can't go around saying it," warned Romeo uneasily.

"Why?"

"Where's our proof? The grave's been fixed up! He'd just deny it and folks'll think I'm crazier than I really am."

Marvin grinned.

"I've got proof and what's more, I know *why* he did it."

"Why?"

"Because he didn't have the guts to hold still!"

That's What Murder Is

Eve had lived just long enough to protest her fate in one smothered gasp and to momentarily realize her terrible mistake.

It could have been hours later that Wayne arose shaking and bewildered, with a first semblance of awareness. Actually, it hadn't been fifteen minutes. But the light was gone. Day's last gleam had tiptoed out, refusing to be witness. The shadows were brooding and deep.

The boy looked about him, still trembling in his stupefaction, and slowly came to realize and understand the huddled bundle of nakedness and torn garments at his feet. He knelt down in terror.

"Eve! Eve!"

Then a vast sob of loneliness and remorse rent him. Stumbling blindly to his feet, he plunged deeper and deeper into the Lodgepole thicket.

An hour later on his way home Romeo found Wayne's body!

Word gets around fast, and sun-up next morning there were some of the citizens at the Federal Building: Seth, of course, Sam Jones, Romeo, Max Shoemaker and Parson

Lambert among others; and a few minutes later, Marvin!

They were sort of waiting for him, and the first thing he did was to take a penny postcard out of his pocket. It was inscribed with pencil in a large, childish, immature school-girl hand.

"It's from Eve Corvell," he said, looking as though he didn't want to read it very much; but after a minute he did.

"Dear Mr. Culbertson: The Yaaters are talking of you coming home from medical school. I want to talk to you. I would like to go Outside and study to be a nurse. We don't have any money; do you think I could get a job Outside? Everybody in the valley acts as though I already belong to Wayne; even Wayne. I don't and I told him so. Maybe you could help me before he does something crazy."

There was a long silence.

"He sure done something crazy," Sam Jones said finally, reaching for his plug cut. Marvin turned the card over and over in his hands.

"I got this in Missoula two days after the stamps were cancelled at the county seat; almost a week after she wrote it."

"That must have been the day the McKinney kids found her body," figured Seth. "And that just gives you some idea of our mail service," he added, getting a plug in for his pet peeve. "The way Uncle Sam don't take care of his Montana kin!"

"Point is," Marvin said, "I hardly knew the Corvells. I didn't even know Eve by sight."

"Kid of twelve or thirteen when you went out to school," nodded Seth. "But she knew you."

"Anyway, I was just breaking up housekeeping in Missoula, and I stuck this card away as neither interesting nor important and forgot it. Last night when Romeo was talking to me about knowing it was Wayne who marred Eve's grave, I remembered." He held out the card to Seth, "For the record!"

Seth took the card reluctantly.

"You figure this tells who killed Eve and why?"

Marvin shrugged.

"And why he trampled her grave?"

"Obviously to make people think some crazy monster was loose up here in the Yaate...killing, raping, desecrating. . . . He felt so guilty he was sure people were looking at him; he had to do something to distract their attention."

"I never even considered Wayne," said Parson. "Any of you folks?"

There was a general shaking of heads.

"The guilty flee where no man pursueth," quoted Seth piously.

"I never *did* understand about murder," Sam Jones said with a troubled, worried expression. "Killing each other always seemed senseless. But more than that, how can folks do it? I mean when you come right down to lifting your hand, how can you look a fellow human in the eye and go ahead with something so brutal and final?"

Nobody had an answer until after some consideration Marvin spoke up:

"The really terrible thing about murder is that mostly it

comes out of the inside of you like a dirty word when you've been hurt or scared; or like doubling up your fist in a flash of anger; it's something that you didn't realize was inside you, and it slips out unintentionally."

"Wayne raped the girl besides!" protested Max Shoemaker.

"Why not? People were saying she was promised to him; already he'd possessed her in fantasy."

Romeo shook his head. "I swear to my grandma, when I cut down through Squaw Crick and Indian Hollow and seen Wayne hanging there on Gallow's Tree, I was plumb sick to my stomach. I thought he'd suicided hisself on account of life wasn't worth living without Eve." He stared at his snoose box with distaste. "And all the time it was because he couldn't live with hisself any longer."

Marvin nodded.

Seth wasn't satisfied! "But if Wayne felt justified in doing what he done," he challenged, "then where's any room for remorse and suicide?"

"That's what unpremeditated murder is: *after* the fact! A mirror of the mind; a sudden unbelievable exposure of what you really are; a self-revealing bloody lust for all the world to look at; for Wayne himself to look at!"

We buried Wayne in the Morgan plot which was right next to the Corvell plot. That brought Wayne and Eve together for Eternity; and in the end Wayne had it his way.

PART VIII

Female Critters

September, 1940

"Man could get hisself clawed to death by a female critter's good intentions."

Romeo McFeddor expectorated tobacco juice past the horse's ear and slapped its rump with the reins over the dash of Hal Morgan's buckboard. He glanced over his shoulder. Mrs. Morgan was still unconscious, her head in Chili Winneger's lap.

"I only aimed to h'ep you get her loaded aboard. Not drive you home. Now I'm missin' the most interestin' buryin' since who laid the chunk."

"She could come around quicker'n I could git word to God," Chili said firmly, "and no tellin' what kinda panic she'll be in."

They were still two miles from the Morgan ranchhouse, out on the upland of Grizzly Flat above the big trees. The edge of the world was far distant and rimmed with snow-peaked Canadian Rockies to the north, the Great Divide to the east, and lesser blue ridges to the south and west. As far as the eye could see in the foreground was Buckbrush and Lodgepole thickets swept by sun and fresh sweet wind.

"I never hear'd such a hurrah at a graveside and right when Preacher Grocer was acomin' to grips with the Devil. Seems like Miz Morgan come frizzle-minded all at once'd."

Chili nodded.

"Her boy Hal snatched her cake of soap and washrag away."

Romeo looked over his shoulder kinda queer.

"Her *what* rag?"

"Miz Morgan ain't bin a-tall well since Old Man Starr was found bottoms up in the crick last year. Fact is she's been poorly since her ma died five years back, when I first come hired-girl for the Morgans."

"Old lady Peebler!" Romeo snorted. "Handmaiden to God and I bet she's made Him tolerable miserable these last five years. She's prob'ly got all Heaven solemn and sanctified by this time."

"I set with her a good bit the last three months, poor soul."

"Talk was, she never seen a patch of her own bare hide in all her days except her hands and face. Washed her person under her nightgown on account the human body ain't fit for human eyes!"

Although Romeo made statements there was a note of inquiry in his voice.

"And feet!"

"Say which?"

"Hands, face and feet was admissible," said Chili matter-of-factly. "Truth to tell, she had Old Man Starr come in and wash her feet night before she died."

"And he done it?" Romeo was incredulous.

"It's Bible."

"What is?"

"Feet washin'! Mary and Martha done it to Jesus. It's Bible."

"So's Absalom gettin' drunk and layin with his two daughters, but that don't make it allowable."

"It wasn't Absalom."

"Whosomever," shrugged Romeo.

"Anyway, Miz Morgan here, after her mother died, began dustin' the furniture twicet sometimes three times a day! In the rest period of an afternoon I've gone to the kitchen and there she'd be with a pan of hot soapy water a re-washin' all the dishes out of the cupboard."

"I can't chamber an overly clean female," Romeo muttered with disfavor.

"Then Old Man Starr died and Miz Morgan took to washin' the cabin walls with soap and water. One night Mr. Morgan heard a noise and come out of his bed. Miz Morgan was in her nightdress on a chair with a pan of water and a rag, washin' the ceiling."

"No wonder Hal Morgan took to liquor."

"Not only that, but when the fambly was asleep she'd sneak in and try to wash 'em. Young Hal let her; him bein' still gander-eyed. He'd lie stiff and wide awake and take his scrubbin'; when she come to Wayne he'd talk to her quiet and get her back to bed, but Mr. Morgan'd wake up with a damp rag on his face and yell fit to turn your hair."

"Her ma must of bin scairt by a Chiny laundryman." Romeo shook his head, "And everybody figurin' the Morgans fer Yaates Valley's number one fambly."

"Then when Wayne hanged hisself over that towheaded Eve last week Miz Morgan really set to work washin' and polishin'. She went through the house like Samson smitin' Philistines."

"That when her old man took to the Ridge?"

"Between Miz Morgan's soap and water and Wayne, Mr. Morgan was a hard-put man."

Romeo nodded.

"Powerful medicine for young Hal."

"Seemed like he paid no attention," Chili said, pondering. "Read a book, pitched in, and helped me milk the cows when his pappy took off. But I guess he just couldn't chamber seein' his mother make a display at the funeral. If she'd got up to the casket with that damp cloth and soap she'd have given Wayne a final wash as sure as sweat in summer."

Romeo was shocked.

"The whole Morgan clan's got leaky skimmers! Wonder what went with the boy when his ma let out that screech and turned on him."

"He slunked off, tail between his legs. We won't see his shadder again today. And that's something else; if Miz Morgan don't come around, you most likely'll have to go for Marvin Culbertson."

"In Grandma's mug!"

"More'n that you prob'ly gonna he'p me with the milkin'."

"Woman," expostulated Romeo grimly, "I kin carry a kindness jus' so far, and we're 'way past the end of the trail right now."

There was a long silence as the buckboard rattled up the last mile of stony road. It was Chili who finally broke silence:

"Then what you bin tellin' folks about Chili Winneger asettin' fire to your foxtail was jus' thistledown on the breeze?"

The back of Romeo's neck turned red clear up into his uncropped hair. He said nothing.

An hour later when Sara Morgan had been put to bed, conscious but still in a sleepwalker's daze, Romeo and Chili went to the barn. Romeo clumb up in the haymow to fork hay down the hay-hole. Chili clumb up to help. The hay was soft and sweet-smelling and the hay-hole had to wait.

Marvin Finds Young Hal

Up along Salt Creek toward Granny Culbertson's, Marvin was sitting on the grassy slope overlooking a shaded open pool with ripples at either end and a tangle of root snags at the bank's edge, where lurked natives, speckled and rainbow trout.

Marvin's back was against a stump, a rod with twenty feet of line drifting in the lower ripple braced in the ground against his buttocks and held steady between his knees. He was absorbed in Liege's *Psychological Approach to Surgery*. Marvin Culbertson (Culbertson only by courtesy of lifelong association with old Granny Culbertson), was a Montana mountain boy long before he'd realized an ambition for scholarship and a doctor's degree; so when a trout struck he sensed it coming and had the pole taut, the fish on the bank and in his creel before it could whisper "Wup!"

When the shadow of young Hal Morgan crept out of the Lodgepole pines and flitted across to the creek side of the road among the big timber, Marvin was aware of that too.

He was conscious of the boy, yet did not stare. The creek separated them, a matter of a few yards, below the pool. Marvin kept his head down as though reading, so that he would not appear to be spying when the boy spotted him.

He was not at all the groomed, decently dressed youth

Marvin had seen with his mother and Chili at the funeral. Mrs. Morgan's fit of rage; drubbing her son with fists, violent in voice as in action; and Hal's attempt to fade away, had been witnessed from among the "standing mourners" by Marvin.

He'd cut around the crowd and caught up, walking beside him for a moment. The boy was blind with an awful shame and paid no heed. Marvin just got in a quick:

"It's Marvin Culbertson, son; I hear you read books; come up Salt Creek and see me—anytime." As the boy broke into a sobbing run Marvin called: "Make it sometime today if you feel amind to."

Apparently the word had got through, for here, five, six hours later was a tired tattered furtive figure. Marvin still wasn't sure Hal was ready for the human touch, but at least the wandering, lost spirit had come up Salt Creek when there were a hundred other directions he might have taken.

The boy was lying on his stomach drinking from a small pool. He put his hot dirty face into the water, gulping long and greedily. Afterwards he lay with his head on folded arms; motionless.

Marvin's heart grieved strangely. He remembered his own adolescent wanderings in these same woods along this same creek, the time it first come home to him that he was not as other boys, but a doorstep orphan whom Granny had succored as she would a wet kitten or an abandoned puppy.

Who he was, what he was, haunted him throughout his growing years; had made him shy, reticent and had turned him to books instead of people.

Not that he didn't love people from afar. He loved everyone; he felt a great caring for them, even as a boy; a great urge to be something helpful in the human family. He had a glowing positive need to reestablish himself, to rectify his outcast, abandoned status, placed upon him by his real parents, who had found no place in their lives or love for him.

As the years wore on and he matured, his understanding widened and he lost most of the bitterness against those who had rejected him. Outside, with the Yaates behind him, he discovered it wasn't always neglect or indifference which separated parent and child; more often social and economic forces entered the picture; sometimes it was death; at times great sacrifices were made by a brokenhearted parent to give a child a fairer chance. So Marvin had made peace with himself and the world.

And now here was another agonizing young spirit, haunted and driven. His older brother, Wayne, a murderer, rapist, and finally a suicide; his mother barely balanced on a silken thread, swaying between reality and her world of grotesque religious fantasy; and his father, Hal Morgan, Senior, supposedly the backbone of both family and community: where was he? Fled to the Ridge in the face of so much disaster, drowned in liquor! Tales came down that he had not had a sober moment in a week; if he kept it up, he'd be dead or a case for the State Hospital in a month.

Maybe it was better not to have parents and family. Maybe! Either way it was a hell of a note for teenagers.

The boy moved; he rolled over on the thick bed of leaves and needles and looked up through the high lacy branches to the sky. He seemed to be calculating escape; measuring just how far away heaven was; or perhaps he was looking to see if there really were Pearly Gates, and if so, whether his Grandmother Peebler and Old Man Starr and . . . and Wayne, might be there somewhere outside the Gates, waiting for St. Peter. Maybe he was even wondering; could and should he take his mother and father with him and, might they all find happiness together up there?

"That's my imagination," Marvin reproved himself, "not his! I never thought of dying or wanting to die in my most despondent moments at his age. No healthy boy does. He's desperately unhappy, unsettled and pretty worn out; maybe he'll sleep a little."

To belie this Hal sat up. In a sudden frustration of revolt and despair his face screwed up in an agony of rage and he beat the ground with his fists. To Marvin it was, in a way, a child having a temper tantrum; or a trapped animal in its final effort of murderous fury, before resigning itself to the inevitable.

Abruptly the boy got to his feet and saw Marvin. He shot behind a giant Cedar. He stood hidden, panting, in a fright. After an interminable time he peered out. Marvin was reading, apparently unaware.

Hal watched! Suddenly the top of Marvin's pole jerked a signal; quick as spring lightning Marvin had the pole in hand and was playing the hooked fish away from the root tangle under the bank. Two minutes more a ten-inch speckled trout was in the creel.

Marvin cast and went back to his reading. If he could have observed he would have seen the weight of a trouble roll off the boy in those two minutes, supplanted by suspenseful awareness of the moment; youthful enjoyment relaxing his face. With Marvin's settling down again, the intent, hopeless moodiness returned. He tiptoed away keeping the big trees between them. When he'd reached another barrier he stopped, turned and cautiously peered back.

He stayed, watching Marvin.

In the end young Hal could not bring himself to go; but

neither apparently could he find the courage to make his presence known. Marvin caught two more trout, both natives, and decided it was time to make his move. He wound his line, broke down his pole and with book and pole in one hand, the creel over his shoulder, he waded the creek in the shallows above the pool and went through the forest toward the Salt Creek road, passing within a few yards of Hal, kneeling, concealed. He paused.

"I'm glad to see you come up Salt Creek," he said, not glancing in the boy's direction. "How about traipsing along to the cabin with me and having fried potatoes, cornbread and all the trout you can eat? And don't worry about me not gettin' my share."

There was a long wait. Marvin was patient. After a considerable interval young Hal came out of hiding a little shamefaced.

"You know'd I was there all the time," he said accusingly.

"Sure!" But the way Marvin put it, it had no sting, wasn't important.

The moment the boy came alongside, Marvin kept him moving, pulling him slowly in the direction he wanted him to go.

"Mind carrying my book a piece?" he invited, thrusting his psychological treatise on surgery into Hal's hands. The boy's face lighted; he handled the book with reverence; the frown on his face evidenced incomprehension as to the subject matter, but it didn't matter. It was a book; precious reading matter; a source of magic; a fund of fabulous information; a well of forgetfulness against dreadful, painful reality.

All this Marvin thought he saw in the boy's face and manner as they walked. Hal's eyes feasted first on the cover and then, with permission, he peeped inside.

"I heard down at the Federal Building that next to me, you're the Traveling Library's best customer," Marvin threw in casually. Then with an attempt to commit the boy, "If you could clean the fish whilst I slice the potatoes and stir up some cornbread, we could eat right soon."

"Don't Granny Culbertson cook for you?"

"Not me!" Marvin was amused. "First place, Granny's now close onto ninety and eats mostly gruel. She's up with the chickens amorning and to bed with the same flock come sundown. Besides that, I'll tell you a secret. Since being Outside three, four years studying medicine, I'm a weensy squeamish about Granny's dirt. When she cooks a meal it ain't exactly done according to the minimum standards set down by the State Board of Health."

"That's no secret," said Hal. "Everybody knows Granny's pig-dirty and sewed in her clothes."

"Maybe," said Marvin, "but underneath her dirty old hide is all the kindness in the world."

Hal looked at him fleetingly out of the corner of his eye.

"A little kindness and fellow-feeling applied at the right time by almost anyone; dirty, clean; friend, stranger; man, woman or child—will sometimes cure the soul of a man momentarily panicked and running away, indeed, may make the difference whether he keeps running for the rest of his life or whether he turns around and licks the situation whilst it's still to his size.

"He *don't* lick it right off it's bound'n to grow into a frightening monster of a shadow that'll blot out the whole world; and all the time it's growing, the man's getting weaker in his will, more fearful, and pretty soon loses all power to save himself."

"You talking about me?" Hal demanded truculently.

"I'm talking about folks in general," Marvin said. "Everybody's the same; only right this moment, I guess I am talking about you, mainly; yes, I guess I am."

They walked in silence to within sight of Granny's cabin. Then Marvin said:

"I always did have you figured for the strong member of the Morgan clan."

"What about my pa?"

"Well what?"

"If my pa can't face what's been goin' on at our place then how can I?"

"Because you're young, got a stout heart, and the whole world ahead of you to win back. Your father's getting along onto sixty; he can't start over. But just think of the sixty years he's already stood up to the world successfully, aren't you willing to credit him with all them good years? And something else; if your father can survive the shock of what's happened; if he don't kill hisself with liquor trying to forget; the pain'll ease up presently and he's liable to sober up and be his old self."

"Even with Ma cuttin' didoes?"

"Your ma's sick," Marvins voice was gentle. "Whether she can be helped is something we might look into. But it ain't your mother who'll bring your father down off the Ridge. That'll be you."

"My pa don't know I'm alive," said young Hal hopelessly. "He thought Wayne was wonderful. I was just out of the bottom of the barrel."

"And you'll still be if you go sniveling and running away. But you turn about, face the folks and do what you can to keep the ranch going, one day I don't doubt you'll have the respect of the community, plus your father back again, and the fact that he's bound'n to realize that all the real strength of the Morgans was after all lodged in his younger son."

They were now at the cabin steps. Marvin handed Hal the creel and took the book.

"You take these to the creek yonder and clean 'em up. I'll go in and set fire to the stove and be ready for the fish in two jumps." Marvin thought of something else. "Look son, how'd a pint or two of milk taste right now before supper? You ain't et for quite a spell."

A gleam came into Hal's eyes. All he said was, "I kin wait."

"Wait? What for?" Marvin took a quart jar and went to the smaller root cellar. Presently he returned, the jar full to the brim with cool, rich milk, yellow with cream.

"Here, drink this whilst you're cleaning fish." As he vanished into the cabin he called, "Don't waste no time. I'm so hungry my stomach claws is reachin' out."

Hal turned up the jar eagerly; it was half-emptied when he took it from his lips. He sighed, wiped his mouth with the back of his hand, took the fish to the creek, got out his "skinning knife" as Romeo would call it, and deftly opened, cleaned and washed the trout, leaving on tail and head. By the time he'd finished he'd also emptied the jar of milk, and Marvin yelled it was time to fry fish.

As Marvin and young Hal sat down, the evening was still bright with reflected evening light. The boy suddenly grew uneasy.

"Now what?" Marvin had been watching for symptoms.

"The cows. Nobody milks them there's gonna be a lot of sick cows. Even liable to ruin some of them."

"Your father don't seem to care."

"Well he'll be madder'n a hornet, he comes home and finds I've ruint his dairy herd."

"You feel that responsible?"

"Course Chili'll do the best she can, but it ain't her place."

"But it is your place?" Marvin persisted with the question.

"It ain't nobody else's, I reckon."

"Well, you feel that way about it, after supper I'll hike over to the ranch with you, and we'll milk 'em."

"On foot?"

Marvin grinned.

"Somehow I never seemed to get to the point of affording other than shoeleather transportation."

Marvin, himself, noticed how easily he fell in and out of the Yaater's vernacular. Sometimes Yaate-style English suited best.

"I know some deer-trail short cuts that'll peel down the mileage considerable."

Hal grinned derisively.

Marvin took up the challenge.

"Oh, so you're saying to yourself, what's that Marvin Culbertson think he can tell me about the Yaate's back trails. Okay, so you've combed these hills like a posse smoking out moonshiners. Well, so've I, young feller, beginning 'way back before you was born. We'll see who's so smart."

Hal didn't laugh out loud but he looked like he wanted to.

Thus did Marvin help Hal win back his faith and steady his young heart, and thus it came about that Marvin probed Hal's secret heart.

Naked as a Whore

It was coming onto ten o'clock and twilight was barely lingering in the West when Chili and Romeo finished separating the milk in the root cellar. Whilst Chili was putting the cream to rest she sent Romeo to the cabin to look in on Mrs. Morgan. Romeo was never one to waste energy on haste. He walked like a man belly-deep in cold water going against the current. But he come back, going for God on Resurrection Day.

"That fool woman's drawed a tubful of well water in the middle of the best room and she's sittin' in it, naked as a whore on Maria's weddin' night."

Chili nodded.

"Makin' herself white for God!"

"What I seen, he'd like her better in winter drawers," Romeo retorted. "You ain't put out?"

"I bin expectin' *somethin'*! Maybe the bath'll cool her mind down some. Turn them ten-gallon cans up on the rack to drain."

"But why'd she have to shove all the furniture out in the yard?"

Chili stared.

"I didn't know she did."

"Well she has! Every stick, even the carpet! The room's as bare as she is."

Chili sighed.

"Maybe you're gonna have to go up Salt Creek and get Marvin after all."

"He ain't no doctor."

"He's closest thing we got."

Romeo eyed Chili's generous hips as she bent to pick up the milk pails.

"You sure are aplowin' a mighty wide furrow against my grass fire."

Chili turned the pails upside down on the rack alongside the milk cans.

"Chore's done. Let's go up."

Chili went into the cabin and Romeo sat down on the steps staring gloomily at the furniture, some on the porch, some in the yard; all helter-skelter like moving day with the house on fire.

Presently Chili came out.

"You're gonna have to come in and lend me a hand."

"This here part of the earth sure is littered with trouble tonight, and I gone and stepped in it."

"She's washed and soaped for the Lord, like I thought. She aims to set in that tub 'til he comes and gets her."

"I'm in favor of letting her."

"The water's stone cold. She don't know wet from windy and's got to be put to bed."

"You're stronger'n ever she is."

"Not with convictions workin' on her side."

"She fight you?"

"No, jus' wedges her back and feet against the sides of the tub and goes stiffer'n a bull cook's apron."

"The critter's naked!"

"Maybe the sight of you'll put shame on her and she'll come quiet."

Romeo grunted, unbudged for a spell. Finally he took out his quid from his cheek, like he always did when entering someone else's house, placed it carefully on the porch rail and got up.

"Hal Morgan come home and kitch me mixing my oats with his wife's corn, I'm liable to see God 'fore she does."

Chili led. Romeo came reluctantly, keeping in the background. Sarah Morgan, seated in the circular wooden washday tub of cold soapy water, stared before her with a fixed, unseeing expression.

"She's hexed," was Romeo's low, tentative opinion.

"Miz Morgan," Chili urged persuasively, "You don't want men folks to see you like this. Let me put this here blanket about'n you and he'p you to bed."

There was no response. Romeo took courage and came

closer.

"Christ, woman, you can't spend the rest of your born days in that tub!"

Sarah didn't hear him.

"You ever hear of Zaccheus?" Romeo asked suddenly.

Chili looked surprised.

"Z's for Zaccheus, he clombed up a tree, his Lord for to see. The tree was tall, he caught a fall, and didn't see his Lord at all."

"What's that for?" Chili asked irritably.

Romeo grinned.

"Same thing could happen to a woman in a tub."

Chili took one of Mrs. Morgan's soapy arms firmly.

"Grab a-holt," she ordered.

Romeo had lost his reticence. In fact, mingling with the better classes in the raw now struck Romeo as an interesting way of life. He got Sarah by the other arm. Together he and Chili heaved, but all that happened was to turn the tub half over, flooding the cabin floor.

"That ain't how to do it," Romeo said disapprovingly, "unless you aim to put her to bed, tub and all."

He bent over the woman, putting one arm around the small of her back, the other around her bent knees and squeezed her in a mighty bear hug, broke the traction, and lifted Sarah up in his arms. The same instant all hell broke loose in Sarah. Her wet soapy body made her slippery as a greased octupussy, only more arms. She wriggled and twisted and flailed out until Romeo tripped over the tub.

He came down on top, got a quick picture of what it looked like from a husband's point of view and rolled over. Chili, ready, whipped the blanket over the both of them and threw herself on top the melee.

•

"Good Christ," yelled Romeo, "I can't take you both on at once."

Chili got the woman's arms wrapped in the blanket and held her in a death grip until Romeo wound the blanket around her legs. He sat on her feet while he pulled off his belt and strapped the tightly-wrapped blanket. One of Hal's belts from the bedroom similarly secured her arms. In this makeshift strait jacket, Mrs. Morgan was carried in and put on her bed. From her fighting fit she had gone into a state of lifeless lethargy.

"Makes you think of a chicken that's give up, and sticks his neck out on the chopping block," said Chili rising from making her mistress' head comfortable.

"Somebody could of made a mint of gold off me this morning, bettin' me I'd be rollin' on the floor with Miz Morgan before night," Romeo grinned. "Now, if he'd wanted to make it Chili Winneger, I'd not of took him up."

"Some folks' minds just naturally run like that! Other folks think about where they're goin' next."

"Such as?"

"Salt Crik to Granny Culbertson's and git the young doc."

"Tonight?" Romeo's protest was a bleat.

"You like it better, you kin stay here and I'll go."

"I ain't beholdin' to the Morgans and neither are you. More than that, Marvin ain't no doctor; not yet he ain't."

Romeo's ears perked up and he looked out the window.

"Now who'd be comin' up here this hour totin' a lantern? You s'pose Hal or the boy's come home?"

Chili opened the front door, Romeo at her heels.

"That you, Chili?" came a cheerful voice from down the path. The lantern swaying and jiggling in the hand of the visitor made pools of yellow about her feet and grotesque, dancing shadows behind her. All of a sudden it seemed darker.

"Creeping Judas, what next?" Romeo muttered.

"Who is it?" Chili asked guardedly.

"The madame; Jennie Loughner!"

"Hush," warned Chili, and called, "Yessum, Miz Loughner! Howdy ma'am!"

Jennie's straight, serene figure was now outlined in the lantern glow and as she came up the steps the light from the cabin interior brought her gray hair, gray eyes and strong pleasant features into full focus.

"How's Mrs. Morgan?"

"She's abed," Chili informed her.

"I was at the funeral—" Jennie noticed the shadowy blobs of scattered furniture and held the lantern high. Then she peered through the door questioningly. An exclamation came to her lips as she saw the half-filled tub and the flooded floor. She looked from Chili to Romeo.

"You looking for trouble, you'll git a lavish of it here tonight," Romeo said sourly. "Me, I've had my stomachful." He made as though to depart.

"What you acting so guilty about, McFeddor?" Jennie's voice was friendly but pointed.

"Goddam it ma'am," exploded Romeo, " always feel guilty when I'm in a whorehouse. Why should a madame make me feel any different?"

Jennie nodded unperturbed; looked at Chili. "We need him any longer?"

"Well, there's seventeen cows to be milked and hayed, night and morning."

"I milk," Jennie said.

"And I was figurin' on sendin' over for Marvin Culbertson. Miz Morgan is doin' fairly poorly."

"Come along and show me." Jennie handed the lantern to Romeo. "You'd better stay around until we figure if you're of any use."

Chili led the way to the bedroom and Jennie closed the door behind them. Romeo eyed the lantern sourly, then went outside, found his quid on the porch rail and sat down.

"Skin *my* hide with a dull knife, will she," he muttered. "No wimmen gonna mommix up *my* life. Specially no off-cast critter like *her*. She charge me with a task and I'm liable to clobber up and drizzle on her."

Wimmen is Wimmen

Romeo's mixed feelings about Jennie Loughner were of long duration, going 'way back before Jennie ever set foot in the Yaate. Every spring of the year Romeo's partner, Linc McCary, in those older, wilder days of hunting, trapping and logging, would take his boodle and head for Seattle.

This started back maybe twenty, twenty-five years ago, when he and Romeo played hell with the fur-bearing animals all winter and then did the same for the girls, come time to return to civilization. Only thing, Romeo never got further than Butte or Kalispell with his money, what with liquor, a redheaded woman or a stud game.

Linc banked his money for Christ's sake! Or at least a part of it and he shunned gambling and saloons like ciffy cats, but he sure did love women. Only thing, he said, if you really liked women there was only one place for them and that was Jennie Loughner's in Seattle.

"Wimmen is wimmen!" was Romeo's argument.

"That's because you're an ignorant man, Romeo," Linc would admonish him sorrowfully. "The whores around these Montana camps is so used up they're jes' tired old feedbags empty of every one of their wild oats."

"There's plenty of young 'uns."

"They ain't whores. They're chippies! And I warn you,

they ain't anything more dangerous than a Montana chippy; a man kin get hisself anything from life in the penitentiary to locomotor ataxia from 'em."

Well, Romeo never got either, but one spring when he and Linc come out of the upper wilderness with their packs of beaver, mink, lynx, fox and martin furs, he let Linc persuade him to handle his money until they could both get to Seattle.

This was two years after Linc took out his homestead claim up on Spider Creek; ten years after the trip when Linc come home with the baby.

That was the damnedest yet! Linc McCary coming in from a woman spree in Seattle with a maybe-three-months-old baby boy in a market basket, like bringing home groceries. And nary a word, except he'd cut Romeo's heart out and make him eat it if he ever opened his mouth. And Romeo never did, figuring the year before Linc had got a girl in trouble and now he was disposing of the consequences. He tried to make a couple of comical remarks and pretty near got his teeth rammed down his throat; and Linc was the man who could do it. Romeo was no fool. He picked a really tough man with his fists for a sidekick, on purpose. Maybe Linc would whip him, but likewise for anybody else outside the corporation.

Romeo didn't even get a good look at the kid and the next day it was gone. Romeo figured Linc had made the usual deal with one of the midwives up on the Ridge: only thing a week later Granny Culbertson up on Salt Creek came along with a young 'un. Romeo was real interested until Linc said a man could get his head blowed off poking around in *that* barrel of dynamite.

Anyway this was ten years before the spring Linc saved Romeo's money and they rode the train from Troy over to Seattle to see what Linc's idea of women was. Only thing, the minute Linc gave Romeo his money in Seattle he got so roaring drunk that when he finally got to Jennie Loughner's house, he got throwed down the stairs and kicked out the front door, ass over teakettle, and told never to come back.

Well sir, that made Romeo mad. It was embarrassing going to a whorehouse and sleeping around with strange women; a man *had* to get drunk, the way Romeo saw it. By God, it was indecent, a man walking up to a place like that with a clear mind and all his faculties. It was like whipping a kid in cold blood when you wasn't mad at him: or laying down to sleep in the gutter, cold sober. It just didn't make no sense and to hell with Jennie Loughner, in fact, to hell with Seattle. Romeo went down and got on the next train, home to the Yaate without Linc.

That was the nearest thing to an argument he and Linc ever had: when Linc finally come home and took Jennie's side of the argument. He even went so far as to say Jennie had the kind of girls you had to be sober to appreciate. Jennie's house was like coming home to paradise and the girls were like them whorries that occupy paradise according to some Oriental religion.

Romeo told him he could keep his Goddamned Whorries; he'd take Kalispell chippies hisself. That was Romeo's first resentment against Jennie.

Anyway, that winter they didn't go trapping, but Romeo helped Linc build his log cabin up on his Spider Creek homestead and fix up a root cellar, smokehouse, and a log barn, only they used it for making their own corn. The Volstead Act had been repealed but their palates was used to the amber mountain liquor and why pay government prices for stuff they didn't like as well.

Romeo's second grudge came when Linc died three, four years ago. Naturally he supposed Linc'd leave the homestead to him. But no! A lawyer feller came out from the county seat and said Romeo'd have to move out; Linc'd left the homestead to Jennie Loughner!

Sitting there on the steps of the Morgan log house in the dark, Romeo's mind rummaged through this past history. He felt he had every reason to have a chip on his shoulder, and he'd always have his stinger about half-out around Jennie! Howsomever, Romeo just was not the energetic type or of a feuding disposition. He could be mean and ornery and drag his feet with the best, because that was negative and effortless; but active, aggressive resentment just wasn't in him.

Besides he didn't want Chili to get her back up at him now that he'd got the combination working. He gave thought to Chili's husband, Willy, but only in passing. Willy had a continual fog on up at the Ridge these days and wouldn't even know what folks was atalking about if he was told. Oh, he'd be told all right! He'd hear, on account everybody heard everything about everybody in the Yaate. It might take a day or two for folks to catch on. Then some eager buzzard'd smell carrion and remark, "Willy'll put a spider in Romeo's coffee, sure as pigs litter. Chili's got Romeo pantin' like a lizzard." And old Seth Bascomb'd scowl and say, "People could mind their own business and cut down on the gossip hereabouts, considerable. Only people never do!"

Romeo grinned as he thought of all the things folks was agonna say.

Chili came out onto the porch.

"I'm fixin' to draw a bite and after you've et, Miz Jennie wants to hold meetin' with you."

"I'm around," said Romeo laconically, "but not for long."

"You'd better be! Word should git around that McFeddor up and left two helpless females with a dying woman, you can go live with the ciffy cats."

"Helpless females," murmured Romeo.

"Females is always helpless when it suits their purpose! And it'll git around."

"That ain't the only word that's gonna git around." Romeo grinned up at her.

"Who's telling what?"

"Christ, woman, who has to tell anything? Folks hear Romeo McFeddor's up he'pin' Chili Winneger with the Morgan Ranch chores and every female from the Federal Building to the Ridge is gonna know all the words *and* the music."

Chili thought about it for a moment. Finally she shrugged.

"Well come in and empty that tub whilst I fry some side meat and eggs. Then start moving the furniture back in."

"Whose back did you bust last year?"

"Little woman like Miz Morgan move it out, big strong feller like you kin most likely move it back."

"No wonder men with wimmen around their necks, take to the Ridge."

Chili already had gone to the kitchen.

Romeo just sat; thinking about the troubles of the world and every last one of them was wimmen!

After he and Chili had eaten off the kitchen table, Romeo went out to the porch steps again. Jennie joined him, sitting on the top step above. There was a spell of uncomfortable silence; that is, uncomfortable for Romeo. Jennie was placidly at ease. Finally Romeo had to say something:

"Chili says Miz Morgan's all of a sudden's that weak she couldn't yell soooey if the hawgs had her down."

"You agin goin' for Marvin Culbertson?"

"What good's it gonna do? Way I figure it, Sarah Morgan's ma soured the critter's disposition 'til it et a hole in her crock, and all the common sense leaked out."

"You a doctor?"

"I ain't and that's a fact," Romeo admitted.

"You even a horse doctor?"

Romeo looked resentfully at the shadowy woman above him, but held his peace. There was another pause.

"You know, McFeddor," Jennie said finally, "of all the Yaates Valley folk, you're the only one who treats me uncivil."

Romeo stirred but said nothing.

"All right, I'm an ex-madame. Is that so unforgiving, long as I live peaceable and don't go burrowin' in other folks' back yards? Is what I was any skin off your nose?"

"I bin a lettin' you be," Romeo muttered.

"That was a mighty interesting remark you made about feeling uncomfortable in a House. If you'd ever been to my place in Seattle you might feel different."

"I was to your place." Romeo's resentment showed.

There was a small exclamation of surprise from Jennie.

"I was throwed down about ten steps and kicked out into the street."

"Then you was making a disturbance."

"I was drunk, sure; man always gets drunk going to a place like that."

"Oh!" Jennie sat thoughtful for a while. "Is that what you hold against me?"

"Well it never whetted my appetite."

Jennie laughed.

"Linc McCary must of bin in love of you the way he stood up to me afterwards."

There was a small gasp.

"What was Linc McCary to you?"

"Good God woman, don't you never take the wax out of your ears?" Romeo exploded. "Me and Linc was teamed up like two seeds, to the day he died, more'n thirty years."

Jennie expelled her breath slowly.

"Then you knew most of Linc's affairs?"

"Everything!" snapped Romeo. "We lived in each other's pocket. We put up every last log and shake, together, on the place you live at; we was close as Sin and Shame, twenty-four hours every day."

"You must have liked the place up on Spider Creek, quite a lot." There was gentle inquiry in Jennie's voice.

"I thought it was mine after Linc died 'til that lawyer feller from Outside come and said otherwise." Romeo's voice was gruff, angry.

"If you had it what would you do with it?"

"Set up there and roll rocks down on mankind."

There was another silence.

"If you knew *all* of Linc's business," Jennie said at last, as casually as she was able, "then isn't there anything else you have to say to me?"

Romeo didn't know what she was talking about. It was apparent; to Jennie's relief.

"Only thing I got to say to you," he said, "is that I just plain ain't agonna traipse up Salt Creek tonight. It's so windin', you can't tell comin' from goin' in the dark."

"Morning'll likely do as well."

Romeo was surprised. He wondered why Jennie was all of a moment so agreeable.

Jennie on her part was wondering how Linc had managed the baby so adroitly that his most intimate friend had been kept unawares. In fact, how the whole community had been mystified. Sometimes, everyone didn't know everything about everyone in the Yaate, she decided.

"You agreeable to stay on and help with the cows?" she asked.

"I s'pose!" His short reply was the soul of ungraciousness.

"We'll make up a pallet for you to sleep on."

"In the cabin?"

"You against it?"

"With three wimmen in there, there won't be room to cuss a cat without gettin' fur in your mouth. I'll make out up in the haymow."

"Suits you, suits us," Jennie said, rising. "Chili and I'll be up with Mrs. Morgan, mostly." She started to enter the cabin and then turned back.

"You ever strapped for money, come and see me," she said.

"I'm always strapped."

"Oh?"

"In fact I'd be money in my pocket if I'd never bin born."

Jennie laughed and went inside.

Romeo grunted.

"It'll be a long, red, curly-haired dog of a winter afore I ask *her* for money," he thought. Still, he suddenly had a comfortable feeling; a satisfaction that, at the moment, he refused to acknowledge.

Hal and Marvin

Marvin had to admit defeat within half-an-hour, on the direct return by deer trails, crossing the ridges and ravines from Salt Creek to Upper Grizzly and Grizzly Flat, where the Morgan Ranch lay high and fertile.

During his three or four years away at medical school he'd forgot what a fund of stamina and resources an active Montana mountain boy builds up. Young Hal had him breathing through his mouth in the first twenty minutes and wheezing like a meeting-house pump organ in thirty.

Marvin called a halt.

"Look," he said, sitting on the steep hillside in the half dark, "the only fire in the Yaate worth this much speed is in the Devil's hip pocket and we're not going to catch up with *him*. I'm sweating like a Sunday rain."

The boy stood beside him trying to hide his triumph.

Marvin took a deep lungful of air, looked at the gander-eyed lad, strong as a new rope and as itchy to get on as a bug on a hot night. He grinned.

"I bit off more'n I can chew," he admitted. "I'm hotter'n a fire in a pepper mill! I know when I'm up against my betters. Crouch a little."

Hal sat on his heels.

"How much more *up*, before we hit level?"

"Half-hour!"

Marvin nodded.

"Well the only way you're going to get me there is to nurse me along. I'm ashamed how fragile city life's made me." Marvin put his hand affectionately on the boy's arm. "I had my nerve challenging you; but you fooled me. Hearing all the gossip about what a bookish boy you were, I didn't figure you to kick up such a dust."

"You charged me to lead the quick way." The boy was faintly apologetic.

"Well I uncharge you!" Marvin's face held comradeship as well as humor. Then more seriously with deliberate intent to draw out the boy:

"Man with your thick and ready constitution could go far in this world. They don't breed boys like you on the Outside. You set your mind to it, I doubt if there was anything you couldn't do."

Suddenly Hal settled down and was extremely quiet, a wall of reserve about him. Marvin looked at him curiously. After a moment he commented, "I see you got ideas."

The boy didn't speak for several seconds. "How'd you get to be a doctor?" he asked.

"I've got about four more years before I can call myself that," Marvin said cautiously.

"When did you start?"

"Well I started *thinking* about it when I was your age."

Hal nodded. Finally he said softly:

"I've been thinking."

"I could tell that," Marvin agreed.

"Only it ain't doctoring."

"Want to tell me about it?"

The boy hesitated. Marvin could see a struggle between the desire to talk and a shy, self-conscious reticence.

"Once when I was maybe thirteen, fourteen an Outlander come into the Yaate to do some fishing," Marvin remembered. "I hired out to him as a sort of guide. Turned out he was a surgeon down from around San Francisco. One night, camping out, he took notice of me and we talked 'way on into the night. First thing, I was telling him my yearnings toward medicine and you know he was real sympathetic. Seems like somebody had helped him when he was young and yearning, and he took pleasure in me the same way. That was when my yearning turned into something I could get my claws into. He even sent me books to study. When you get down to it, there's a heap of men with fellow-feeling for them that's trying to get their first toe-hold."

There was another silence. Of a sudden Hal said, "The Yaate's overrun with trouble."

"Oh?"

"I don't mean body sick: I mean the kind of trouble you'd think the Rev. Mr. Grocer'd be minding."

Marvin's breath sucked in. He had to grit his teeth to keep the boy from seeing his reaction. Apparently Hal was waiting for him to say something.

"You want to be a preacher?"

Hal shook his head.

"It ain't the way."

"Let's talk about it," Marvin encouraged.

Hal hesitated and then blurted, "My Ma's troubled with something that's driving her crazy; my Pa's up on the Ridge drinking hisself to death; something made Wayne kill a girl and then go hang hisself."

"I know!" Marvin was all gentleness.

"Even my Grandma Peebler was daft about God and Old Man Starr couldn't talk about anything except Sin and ever-lasting punishment. He sure was a glutton for wantin' God to punish folks.

"Seems like everybody around the Ranch was being driven and lashed 'til they was lathered. And they was so grievous unhappy.

"At first I thought it was just us, but when you look around the Yaate, it seems like it's everybody."

"It's not confined to the Yaate either, son," Marvin said, with awed wonder at the boy's comprehension. "It's all through the Outside too, spread all over the world, seems like."

"What is it?"

"Folks have lost the way."

"You mean the Rev. Mr. Grocer's way?"

"No! He's lost the way too. That's why you were right in

saying, being another Rev. Grocer isn't enough."

"They ought to be somethin'." The boy said it with a conviction. "They sure ought to be, and if there was, that's what I'd like to do."

Marvin tingled and a great joy swelled within him. He wanted to hug the boy to him. Here was a dedicated soul. Misery hadn't frightened, beaten him nor embittered him. It had only given him an amazing insight; a determination; a vision. He felt such a fellow-feeling for this boy it choked him. He didn't dare give way. His excitement would have embarrassed Hal. All he said was:

"There is something! There's a great new medical science that's devoted entirely to just what you're talking about."

The boy's eager eyes searched his face. It was so dark now he had to lean in close to Marvin, giving a tense, alert, forward thrust to his head and shoulders, as a thirsty animal who scents water.

"What do I do?"

"Study! Give the next twenty years to learning. It's a long, hard intensive work, but if it's what you want you'll find such happiness as you've never known."

"How do I start?"

"Finish your general education; then a medical education; finally training in psychiatry."

"In what?"

"That's this new medical field I'm talking about. The study of people's minds and emotions; all the drives and forces inside which make people think and feel and act as they do. Come to an understanding with yourself, that'll make it possible to help these troubled people."

"It could help Ma?"

"Twenty years ago it might have; now I don't know. What's been haunting your mother is so longstanding it could be chronic. Like a disease that started as an infected finger and was let go until the whole arm is destroyed."

"And it could have kept Wayne from...from doing what he did?"

"If he'd been helped when he was a young boy, yes."

Hal sat silent. Presently he said:

"Could you show me the way?"

Marvin held out his hand.

Hal looked surprised, then took it tentatively.

"I've got me a younger brother, tonight," Marvin said, happier than he dreamed he would ever be. "You want me to show you the way, you got yourself a guide!" He laughed! "Only with your stamina I'd better watch out or first thing I'll be panting along behind you, like climbing this trail."

Hal listened and then withdrew his hand shyly, but he hadn't missed a word and Marvin knew it had been burned into his soul. He sensed enough had been said.

"Well," he said, rising, "if we're going to get those cows milked tonight, we'd better step on the cat's tail."

Marvin looked up at the sky. A great evening star was showing above the white craggy peaks of the Canadian Rockies. He wished on it. He wished that he might be worthy to guide this sturdy, simple, yearning, young mind.

Voice from the Hayloft

Romeo had barely wallowed a nest for himself in the hay when the barn below was filled with lantern light and voices came up to him. He reared up on his elbow and by God, the first voice he heard was young, almost-a-Doc, Marvin Culbertson, come out of the blue; as though Chili's and Jennie Loughner's talking about him had conjured him up. Then he heard the boy's voice. Not the sick dog-with-a-thorn-in-his-foot kid he'd seen at the funeral, but normal as a cob and full of wonder.

"Will you looky at what Chili Winneger's done all by herself!" he heard young Hal exclaim. "Milked all the cows; throw'd hay out of the mow; even got the mangers full for morning."

"That Willy Winneger's wife?" came Marvin's voice.

"That's queer!" There was a bubble of amusement in Hal's voice.

"Queer?"

"Chili's been eatin' away at Willy goin' on five years; it's her main gossip and always down her nose; you know, like as though cholery was over the next rise, blowin' this direction. But I never once *seen* Willy. I had to stop and remember he wasn't just some of her story talk."

"Chili must be a worker."

"She flings around like a bug on a hot fire. Her tongue aflip-flappin' constant but so is her hands and all the rest of her. You never seen Chili?"

"Never to notice!"

"Well you should ought to. Her breasts look like another pair of arms, cut off at the elbow under her apron. Old Man Starr used to say if she'd attach hooks to 'em she'd have four hands."

Marvin laughed.

Hal's voice grew suddenly warm and apologetic. "You can't make fun of Chili, though; she's kinda like a settin' hen up here scratchin' for the Morgans; Ma clings to her."

"Seems I've been missing something."

"Seventeen cows is a heap of milking!" The boy couldn't get over his admiration. "I don't know how she done it."

Romeo had a growing irritation up in the mow. After all he'd milked ten of the seventeen and more'n that he'd throw'd down all the hay.

"Maybe somebody come by and lent her aid," Marvin suggested.

Hal shook his head.

"I think Chili laid out to do this job herself."

"Like hell!" Romeo roared down the hay chute.

Marvin grinned.

"Looks like you got company in your guest room."

"Some folks don't know from Chiny." First Romeo's feet showed on the hay-hole ladder, then a pair of long shanks in red flannel drawers and finally Romeo himself.

Hal's eyes bulged. Marvin was between amusement and disbelief. Romeo dropped to the floor, stomped through the manger hay and ducked under a stanchion, still indignant.

"Folks whose noses is mostly betwixt the lids of a book seldom know up from sideways," he challenged.

"You've been helping Chili with the chores?" Marvin asked in disbelief.

"Somebody had to keep the Morgan place pulled together," Romeo replied truculently, "what with Miz Morgan goin' puny, Old Man Morgan Ridge-bound and the boy here letting a shuck for tall timber."

Marvin put his arm around young Hal's shoulders protectively.

"It was neighborly of you," he said quietly.

Romeo looked from one to the other and some of the fire went out of him.

"Nothin' of the kind," he muttered. "Chili got her claws into me. I was lashed to the job afore I could defend myself."

The boy had stood bewildered, taking it all in. Now he inquired gratefully:

"You was staying the night, to help in the morning?"

"Seems like." Romeo, caught red-handed doing a kindness, felt ill-disposed.

"Thank you."

"No thanks due," Romeo denied. "Like I say, I was tricked into it. What with Chili hawg-tying me and Jennie Loughner showin' up to put in her two-bits worth."

"Jennie Loughner's here?" Hal's surprise was renewed.

"Yonder in the cabin."

Marvin looked at the boy and smiled.

"Looks like you got friends in the Yaate, son."

A flush spread over the boy's face.

"Maybe you best go up," Romeo suggested. "Both Chili and Jennie was a-yappin' at my heels to go fetch you. But seein' you're only a half-baked doc so far, I didn't heed 'em."

Marvin grinned. "You're probably right."

"Just the same, now you're here you'll save me the trouble of goin' to fetch you in the morning."

"You want to come along, Hal?"

"Why don't he stay here?" Romeo asked.

Marvin looked at Romeo questioningly.

"Seems like Miz Morgan needs more care'n a preacher in poor health."

Marvin sensed Romeo's meaning. "I won't be long."

Hal appeared to have no desire one way or the other. When Marvin's shadow disappeared in the direction of the lighted cabin, he crawled into the manger and lay down on the hay as though Romeo didn't exist.

Romeo scratched himself, stood on one foot and then the other. If he wanted to say something comforting he had no facility for it. Finally he moved to the hay chute, saying more to himself:

"Well if you're gonna usurp the downstairs bedchamber, I'll clomb back up. I could quit sleepin', but it makes agin me."

Hal didn't move.

Marvin Meets Jennie

Chili answered the door. She was in a wrapper, tied severely around her waist, which drew it tight across her chest. Marvin saw immediately what young Hal had meant. She looked as though she were hiding two loaves of French bread under the garment.

Her expression, which combined behind-the-door-conspiracy with a warning protest, showed she'd expected Romeo. The sight of Marvin flabbergasted her; for a second she gobbled. Recovering, she threw open the door and fairly sucked him in; giving Marvin the sensation of being pulled inside by an irresistible vacuum.

"My land! It's Providence come home to roost," she fluttered. "Me and Miz Loughner's at our minds' end. The Devil sure has got Miz Morgan by the short hairs on a downhill pull. Miz Loughner's settin' with her yonder in the bedchamber. You know Miz Loughner?"

"By name," Marvin said. "She came into the Valley about the time I went Outside to school."

"She's a nice woman, Miz Loughner, even if she did play Little Bo Peep to a flock of loose women for twenty-five years. You'd natcherly s'pose a woman like that'd give you the feelin' that skunks'd littered under the cabin. Nothin' of the kind; she's as clean-minded as a spit of a girl that's still harmless."

Marvin grinned.

"You want to go in and tell her I'm here?"

Chili did want to. She fairly skittered. In a moment Jennie came out. She closed the door behind her and for a moment stood rigid, feasting her eyes on Marvin. Her expression was so intense, Marvin suddenly felt exposed and extremely uncomfortable; a faint flush came to his cheeks.

"Miss Loughner?"

Jennie recovered, nodded and smiled and held out her hand.

"Well it's time I met Marvin Culbertson. The way the Yaaters hold you up to praise, made me a little taken aback for a moment."

Marvin doubted that. This woman had character, poise, steady eyes, a no-nonsense handgrasp and a warm, pleasant personality that appealed to him strangely. He looked at her curiously. In fact he looked at her with wonder. He'd seen a few madames on the Outside, but none like Jennie Loughner. She reminded him more of the matriarch of a large well-adjusted family.

"You know I'm not allowed to practice medicine," he said.

To herself Jennie was saying, "What a fine man; what a good man! Thank you Lord." Aloud she said:

"Any knowledge any of us has, out here away from help, is allowable." She couldn't help that proud, happy emotion. It was like standing in the presence of a miraculous achievement.

"Of course," agreed Marvin.

"We're neighbors of a sort," Jennie said out of nowhere.

"Maybe you'll come up Spider Creek on an occasion and get better acquainted."

"Thank you!" Marvin smiled. This woman had a kind of graciousness he couldn't fathom, and no desire to resist. He most certainly would go up Spider Creek. "By the way," he remembered, "I brought young Hal home with me."

Jennie looked concerned.

"I fed him. He's waiting out in the barn with Romeo."

Jennie turned to the bedroom door; Marvin followed.

Chili rose from the bedside where she'd been chafing Sarah Morgan's hands.

"She's in some kind of a conniption for sure," she said as Marvin knelt beside the unconscious woman.

"I've seen a lavish of death in my time," the mountain woman went on, "and the sign's on Miz Morgan for sure."

Jennie began a gesture for silence, met Marvin's amused wink and refrained. Chili's third pendulum was loose.

"My experience has run from wrecktle injuries on the highway, which took my first husband Ace to the bosom of God, to a hearty condition which took Jack Lucey and left me a widdy-woman on my second honeymoon. In betwixted and between I've put two cousins in Institutions for the Mindful, besides losing my first child from me dryin' up and the wet nurse bein' young and buxom and a fresh married girl, who was more interested in beddin' her man than in sucklin' a paid baby. So natch'ly he didn't last."

Chili was in her element. Here was a doctor man whose business was birth, death and all the in-between details of human weaknesses; she didn't intend to leave out a thing.

Marvin looked up from counting Sarah's pulse and said to Jennie:

"I don't like leaving the boy alone too long; if I'm going to make any kind of an examination it may take time."

Jennie understood, nodded and went out. Chili had no intention of leaving.

"My twins was born with their return-trip tickets in their pockets; the Angels took 'em right out of the midwife's hands so to speak. Pa said it was best on account I was an abandoned woman at the time; Ace having left my bed and board. Pa lasted 'til just a couple of years ago; strong all his life 'til suddenly he began to go. Only thing wrong his whole life was weak gum-bones; always was a teether; so he had 'em all yanked out when he was twenty. Later, he had some communion with a Crochety Specialist over some hem-stitching of his rectitude; piles we call 'em."

Marvin, without either thermometer or stethoscope was doing his best at rough and ready examination. He'd had his ear against Sarah's chest, listening to her uncertain breathing when Chili came forth with her father's grievance. He snorted and choked and buried his face in his hands to keep his laughter to himself. He looked at Chili as though he were kneeling in worship.

"Prayer the only thing kin he'p her?" she asked anxiously.

Marvin recovered.

"I was just thinking," he said. "What happened just before Mrs. Morgan went into this coma?"

"Why she threw a fit and me and Romeo had to rope and tie her."

"Oh?" Marvin rose and sat on the edge of the bed. "Tell

me about it."

"Ain't much to tell. We come home from the funeral; Miz Morgan was some dazed so's I put her to bed. Then me and Romeo went out to milk, we come back, Miz Morgan had moved all the furnishings out of the next room into the yard and was sittin' naked in a washday tub of well water, lavin' and soapin' herself pearly white for God."

"She said that?"

"Only thing she did say! I tried to git her back to bed but she braced her knees and back agin the tub, so I got Romeo and he lifted her out. Only all a sudden she was all over him like a treeful of wild cats and it throwed him and down he went on top of her. He rolled right off, keepin' it decent, and I was standin' by with a blanket which I throwed over her. We laced her up tight with a couple of belts and put her here on the bed."

"When did she go limp?"

"Exact minute escapes me, but shortly after she and Romeo took the fall."

Marvin went back to his knees and began to examine Sarah's head and neck. In a moment he exclaimed and then gently rolled the woman on her side. There was a deep bruise from which a tiny ooze of black dried blood showed.

Chili had gone back to her saga of family ills and was paying no heed.

"Me, I was never a peaked girl myself, 'cept for a eary condition with mastadons and later a corny disposition of the feet."

"Chili!" Marvin's tone commanded her attention. "This woman has a concussion; might even be a fractured skull;

look here!"

Chili obediently knelt.

"Now, however did she do that to herself?" she exclaimed sympathetically.

"You said she fell."

"I've taken worse falls'n that since I was fifteen—"

"This woman's got to be rushed to a hospital."

"Kalispell's eighty miles—"

Marvin cut her off.

"The Morgans have a light truck. I'll go back it up to the door. You get a couple of mattresses ready for the truck bed; also plenty of blankets or sougans to keep her warm." He moved out of the room quickly.

Chili shook her head.

"He's sure enough a doctor," she said disapprovingly. "Always wantin' folks to die in a hospital 'stead of their own bed, the way the Lord provided."

Chili was right. The truck with Marvin at the wheel, young Hal beside him and Jennie seated on the edge of the mattresses behind with Sarah, hadn't reached the top of the grade, twenty miles on their way, when Jennie tapped on the cab's rear window.

Marvin hopped out and climbed into the back. One glance confirmed it. Sarah had gone to God.

The news of his wife's death sobered Hal Morgan and brought him down from the Ridge. The ranch had an air of abandonment. Chili was there and so was Romeo; the dairy stock sufficiently attended. But without Sarah, Wayne and Old Man Starr, yes, and even Grandma Peebler, it wasn't the Morgan Ranch any more. He wandered about aimlessly. It was a couple of hours before he thought to ask about young Hal.

"He's went up Salt Creek to stay with Marvin Culbertson," Chili told him.

"Any particular reason?"

"The boy's took to Marvin. Follows him like a sucking pup under its mama's feet. You quit the Ridge for good?"

Hal looked at Chili with burning eyes.

"Well a person can't be hung for askin'," Chili bridled. "McFeddor's restless to git back to his settin' and whittlin' and I ain't had wages for three weeks now."

Hal reached for his purse, fished out several bills and thrust them at Chili.

"You're paid," he said ungraciously, "and tell McFeddor to go mind his own business. You go with him."

"There's a grateful heart for you," said Chili resentfully. "Who's gonna git your victuals?"

The owner of the Morgan Ranch didn't answer. He turned on his heel and stalked off.

The first Yaaters knew, several big trucks from a dairy ranch over near the county seat lumbered up Grizzly Flat and drove off with the milk cows. A month later the rumors had it that the Morgan place had been sold to a Spokane Gun Club and quail, partridge, grouse and pheasants were being planted by the thousands. Some reports even exaggerated there was to be a private landing field for airplanes.

There'd be Outlanders in and out of the Yaate henceforth like openin' the Gates of Hell. The natives were bitterly resentful. The whole blamed Valley suddenly'd gone to pot with the wasting away of the Morgan Clan.